ISLE OF
DREAMS

ISLE OF DREAMS

KEIZO HINO

TRANSLATED BY CHARLES DE WOLF

Dalkey Archive Press
Champaign and London

Originally published in Japanese as *Yume no shima* by Kodansha, Tokyo, 1985
Copyright © 1985 by Keizo Hino
Translation copyright © 2009 by Charles De Wolf
First edition, 2010

Library of Congress Cataloging-in-Publication Data

Hino, Keizo, 1929-2002.
[Yume no shima. English]
Isle of dreams / by Keizo Hino ; translated by Charles De Wolf. -- 1st ed.
    p. cm.
ISBN 978-1-56478-603-6 (pbk. : acid-free paper)
I. De Wolf, Charles. II. Title.
PL852.I47Y8613 2010
895.6'35--dc22
                          2010028394

Partially funded by the University of Illinois at Urbana-Champaign and by a grant from the
Illinois Arts Council, a state agency

This book has been selected by the Japanese Literature Publishing Project (JLPP), an initiative of the Agency for Cultural Affairs of Japan

www.dalkeyarchive.com

Cover: design and composition by Danielle Dutton
Printed on permanent/durable acid-free paper and bound in the United States of America

1

When our consciousness begins to change, for better or for worse, events around us seem to fall into line, starting with mere coincidences, hardly worth noting. Of course, how could it be otherwise?

It was just after noon on a clear day in early spring. The trees along the avenues of the business district, in the center of the metropolis, not far from Tokyo Bay, had not yet sprouted any visible new growth. Sunk in shadows between the high-rises were still traces of cold air, but out in the sun, particles of light had begun frolicking with all the exuberance of life restored. A southerly wind sweeping through the streets stealthily brought moist air to the creases and countless tiny holes in the hard, dry asphalt surface.

On the sidewalks, men and women office workers on their lunch break passed to and fro. The rays of the sun sparkled—particularly on the lively laughter of young female clerks and on the edges of the magnificent first-floor show windows displaying high-fashion clothing and accessories.

It was the first truly springlike day, but in that business district at noontime there was otherwise nothing out of the ordinary.

As always, Shozo Sakai had gone from the construction firm where he worked to eat lunch in the basement Chinese restaurant of a building two blocks away and then enjoyed a short walk. Although already over fifty, he had not yet put on an ounce of fat, nor had his digestive system weakened with age. He took his daily stroll not for exercise but rather for the uplifting pleasure of passing by the many high-rises along the way.

Tokyo had its share of large office buildings—drab, makeshift affairs, hastily thrown together after the war, usually alongside the so-called second-generation constructions built with some idea of design in mind. Here, however, everything was new, each endeavor having its own touch of individuality. Shozo was not indifferent to the charm of the quaint and stately pre-war structures that had survived the air raids, but he was invariably struck by the beauty of contemporary buildings, sharply geometrical in form, devoid of superfluous décor, adroitly bringing to the fore a texture that was both mineral and metallic.

Particularly when at dusk, the rain having lifted, he happened to see the clouds suddenly part and the sunlight break through the air like streams of golden arrows to illuminate the walls and windows of the high-rises, row upon row, he found himself, quite involuntarily, trembling with emotion.

Now, the noon sun had nothing extraordinary about it, none of the unexpected light effects of morning and evening. Yet the buoyant mood imparted to him by the delightful clarity of this midday respite took him farther down the street than was his habit.

He thought of nothing in particular, nor did he reminisce. He looked up into the sky; already it had begun to relinquish its winter harshness. Then, having thrown a cursory glance at the profile of the show-window mannequins, their heads slightly cocked to one side, he peered at the reflection of a building in the polished hood of a black automobile. As he again looked straight ahead, the building itself suddenly appeared directly before him.

This was not everything that he saw. There were the rough reddish-brown walls of a trust bank, the golden arabesque pattern surrounding the thick glass door, the dappled bark of the trees lining the street, three female office workers walking by together in bluish uniforms . . . Though nothing appeared out of the ordinary, it somehow looked like a double-exposed photograph, another scene having been superimposed.

In the dull, weak light of impending dusk on a cloudy day, there are rows of dark-red brick buildings—all equally squat and solid. From between the walls jut cement-coated posts, ravaged by wind and rain, with likewise weather-blanched, gray granite steps at each entrance, flanked by round stone pillars. On each edifice there is a copper plate embedded in the redbrick wall; on one of them he can make out the words "Mitsubishi House #21."

Here one can read free of charge newspapers, magazines, pamphlets, and books from the Soviet Union. There is no large reading room; the windows are small. The yellowish light of a tungsten lamp illuminates the cool, coldly hushed and stuffy interior. He can see the cover of a large-formatted journal: unadorned, powder-blue, poor quality paper. He recognizes the title printed in cobalt ink: ОКТЯБРЬ. Named for the October Revolution, it is the organ of the Soviet Writers' Union.

It took him by surprise, but not such as to leave him standing breathless on the pavement. As unexpected as the vision of the redbrick buildings and the dark blue Russian letters had been, it had also seemed quite natural—and had vanished as quickly as it had appeared.

As a student just after the war, he had indeed sought out Mitsubishi House #21 and on a few occasions visited the Soviet Cultural Center to read literary magazines. After graduating, however, he had not had anything to do either with the Soviet Union or with literary magazines, and he had seldom thought of it, even after his company had moved to this area some ten years before. He had had neither reason nor occasion, then or now, to give such meaningless matters of long ago any further thought. By nature, he was not strongly inclined to indulge in nostalgia, and since his wife's death from a sudden illness three years before, he had come all the more to regard the past as forbidden territory. In his mind's eye he had just seen the title of the journal as vividly as if he had been holding it in his hand.

Yet he actually felt not the slightest yearning for it—neither for this place nor for his former self.

He attempted to think calmly, but he sensed his exuberance of a moment before fading, though this had neither to do with the Soviet Union nor with his years as a student. He was rather haunted by the eerie intuition that something unexpected had broken into this new urban neighborhood that he had come to see as his own exclusive world.

It was ridiculous for a grown man to allow himself to be perturbed by such trivialities. Nothing had, in fact, happened. Yet even as he told himself this, the feeling grew within him on his way back to the office that, little by little, fissures had sprung up in his perception of reality, a perception that hitherto had quite naturally led him to assume a tacit understanding between the district and himself.

A dinner arrangement for that evening had been postponed. Shozo called to a younger coworker preparing to leave, "Care to go out for a bite?"

Outside they waited for a taxi. On the street that at noon had been teeming with passersby, there were now but a handful. The days had grown longer. The lights in the office buildings were already illuminated, but the twilight lingered, tinged with that bluish color that lies at the bottom of shallow water.

He found particularly beautiful the illumination of the aligned windows rising more than ten stories above the ground. "I enjoy looking at these buildings in the evening, with all their rows of lights," said Shozo as they rode in the taxi. "It spoils it for me when they start turning them off as the night wears on. I wonder why. After all, that's when they appear in their purest form, with none of the superfluity of bustling crowds or of the buildings' varying colors. It's obviously not that I'm admiring the people working late. I don't care at all about what is going on behind the windows; I simply find them beautiful."

"Like nighttime New York."

"Yes, perhaps. Once after the war, I saw a night view of New York in a movie and had the feeling of glimpsing another world." It occurred to him that New York might have hardly changed since then.

"I can imagine. Of course, I hadn't even been born then."

"Yes, it was like a dream—yet now we have managed to make it a reality, with our own hands. Our own company has constructed some of the buildings we're seeing around us."

"Here we are," said the young man matter-of-factly. The taxi suddenly came to a halt. Shozo got out of the taxi and was trying to get his bearings, when he was struck and almost blown over by a gust of wind from above.

"It's coming from over there," said his subordinate, looking up and pointing to the other side of the street. Towering some thirty floors into the indigo-blue sky was a new building, its rows of small windows burning brightly.

"The turbulence is terrible!" Shozo thought he knew all about the whirling winds at the base of skyscrapers, but he had never personally experienced anything of this intensity.

"The buildings create this sort of rough air," said his companion. "And they block radio waves as well."

In addition to the high-rise, there were a few shabby multi-tenant buildings of three or four stories, along with shops and modest eating establishments, their advertising signs swaying and clattering. Women pattered by, holding down their hair with a free hand. The wind grew stronger, changed direction, then, after a lull, picked up all the more intensely again. For Shozo, it was as if an invisible barrier were restraining him. "It's up there!" said the younger man, pointing to an alley that lay before them. Bending his head, Shozo hurried breathlessly toward it.

They had all but thrown themselves into the Japanese-style bistro. As they sat down at a table, Shozo felt that they had passed over the border into another realm of existence.

"It's hard to believe that you would find something like this right under a skyscraper!" he exclaimed in genuine astonishment.

"That's Japan for you," said the other. "We construct ultra-modern buildings right over places like this."

Houses of wood and paper, frail huts that might come crashing down—were they not leaning on one another, built as though designed to grovel on the earth in obedience to gravity?—and over these Shozo and his generation had constructed soaring towers of steel and concrete that stood on their own strength alone. And they would go on building more and more.

"By the way, what sort of place do you live in?"

He had meant to inquire about the location, but the young man replied, "In a housing complex. I'm a renter."

"Couldn't you buy a company-built condo at a discount?"

"I could, but it would still be expensive. And I have no desire to wind up saddled with a mortgage for the rest of my life. Of course, my apartment is nothing but a concrete box, exactly like all the others, one stacked on top of another. There are times when I get totally fed up with it, especially in the summer, when I open the windows and happen to see the same sort of living room, with the same sort of furniture, in the wing across the way. The people there are even watching the same TV programs. But I suppose a condo wouldn't be much different."

For Shozo and his contemporaries, buildings of steel and concrete were a goal in life, but for the next generation, they were no more than a starting point.

"Yes, I suppose so," muttered Shozo. It was also likely that the high-rise area that he found so moving, so exciting, was seen with quite different eyes by the young.

"I wonder when the Soviet Cultural Center disappeared. It was located quite near the company." He suddenly found the words to express the thought that had been in the back of his mind since lunchtime.

"Was there such a place? In *our* neighborhood?"

"Yes. One could read Soviet newspapers and magazines—and all for free."

"It's somehow hard to imagine *you* frequenting such a place."

"In university, I took up Russian, more or less on a whim. I wouldn't say 'frequented'; I just popped in from time to time."

"I'd be glad to look into what became of it. Should be easy enough to find out."

"No, it's not worth going that far. It's just that I happened to remember . . ." Shozo felt unsteady. He was not a weak drinker, but now his head was throbbing, as though he could hear the blood coursing through his temples. In the confined space of the bistro, the cacophony of conversation and laughter filled his ears like the roar of ocean waves.

"Is something the matter?" asked his companion, looking at him with concern.

"I have a slight headache."

"You're exhausted. You know, you're overworked. You should take time off, unwind."

Shozo remembered that his interest had been neither in the Soviet Union nor in the Soviet Writers' Union journal. It was rather that this was the only commercial district that had been spared in the air raids. From today's perspective, the edifices were crude, hardly worthy of being called office buildings. Yet where all else was bombed-out ruins and barracks, they had at least robustly endured in their original form.

He felt a boundless longing for those streets, for their regular rows of windows in which the lights were still burning. Here, where he now sat, was itself an air pocket in the turbulence.

"Well anyway, let's go," he said.

2

One Sunday afternoon, Shozo rode a bus to the Ginza, thinking that he would have a late lunch or an early dinner there.

Even on Sundays and holidays there was traffic on the streets, but it lacked the bloodthirsty impatience of a normal weekday afternoon. This made it possible to look out on the passing neighborhoods with a measure of tranquility. Especially since becoming a widower, Shozo would spend his days off taking the bus and touring Tokyo. He was bound to find somewhere along the way a new high-rise or a condominium complex of unusual design. Sometimes, after the bus had passed such a building, he would get off and walk back for a longer and closer look.

So many children! He was struck by the thought as the bus stopped at Sukiyabashi, near Yurakucho Station, and a dozen or so got on all at once. They were mostly of middle-school age, but there were preteen primary-school as well as high-school pupils, boys and girls in equal numbers.

He considered whether they might be on their way to a rock concert, but there was no major venue in this area. Moreover, they were not dressed for such an occasion, and their behavior did not match such a mood. Neither their clothing nor their hairstyles stood out and, far from boisterous, they were remarkably subdued, even whispering as they spoke to one another. Shozo, who normally had no contact with young people this age, was suddenly curious.

At the same time, he felt an urge to go on to the terminal stop at Harumi, where he had not been in some time. He did not get off in the Ginza as intended. Here too children boarded the bus, and he was nearly the only adult remaining as it again departed.

Shozo thought Tokyo was at its most beautiful when glimpsed from the end of Harumi Wharf. It was the same with Manhattan, as viewed from the harbor. Beyond the ever blue-black rolling surface of the bay, the high-rises surrounding Tokyo Tower were all that could be seen. He had often gone on solitary sojourns to the wharf and stood gazing at the urban silhouette until darkness fell. Each time there were more buildings. The sight of the burgeoning capital bolstered his spirits.

The bus had passed Tsukiji, crossed Kachidoki Bridge, and was already in Tsukishima, when Shozo became aware of teeming schoolchildren, all around the same age and all headed in the same direction as the bus. There were even more as they came to Harumi. From the broad avenue, otherwise devoid of vehicles, the bus turned right into a lot lined with warehouse-like buildings and came to a halt alongside a strangely shaped building resembling an immense, metallic bowl turned upside down. The lines walking along the street vanished into it, as though drawn by suction. As the children got off the bus, Shozo found himself following them.

If it was an exhibition, he thought, there would be a sign at the entrance of the building, which was as large as a stadium. But there were no billboards, banners, or even a reception desk to be seen. The children were nonetheless streaming in.

With no other adult in sight, Shozo felt out of place, but as no one was paying any attention to him, he followed them in. Beneath a high-arched ceiling lay a vast enclosed space, without a single pillar, and everywhere there were young people, easily exceeding ten thousand. It did not seem to be a concert or a show that had brought them. Rectangular desks had been neatly aligned to form blocks, on which lay magazines and pamphlets, apparently for sale. The vendors sat inside the enclosures on portable chairs, as endless streams of buyers passed between the rows.

It was an amazingly quiet multitude. Some of the vendors called out, "Only one hundred yen!" or "Mega-interesting!" But they were not shouting. As Shozo stealthily glanced over the shoulders of the children at the desks, he saw cartoon-sketch stories printed on cheap paper, a style these days more likely to be called comics than manga. This was apparently a young people's fanzine bazaar.

He walked around for a while but saw no sign of other adults, nor even university-age youths. Had these boys and girls, middle-school or at the most early high-school pupils, quite on their own managed to arrange for this venue and to attract this massive turnout?

Milling about in the passages were children in a variety of costumes, appearing as television monsters, space aliens, animals, heroes and princesses from fairy tales and myths. Some were garbed and helmeted as Nazis, others as Chinese People's Liberation Army soldiers. There were girls in military uniforms, carrying semi-automatic rifles, and boys dressed as princesses. The guises and disguises had been meticulously planned and executed. With deadly earnest faces, neither shy nor playful, they were drifting about in their own world of fantasy. Not one appeared aware that he, an adult, had strayed into their midst.

However strange the scene, he found nothing the least unhealthy about it. These children had sought out this venue to bring their dreams to life.

And yet there was something about these costumed boys and girls, roaming aimlessly, that clung to them like a dismal shadow. Had Tokyo's neighborhoods become such dreadful places that it was only here, on this artificial island, that these children could act out their fantasies? It was, after all, he and his contemporaries who had produced that same metropolis.

Perhaps if he had had contact with children, he might not have been so astonished. But surely most of the parents of this unbelievable multitude had no idea of what their offspring were so seriously engaged in doing here?

Feeling uplifted, without knowing why, Shozo slipped out of the hall. Not far in front of him, at the end of the island, he could see a park. He crossed the wharf's freight area, empty except for a few parked trucks, and headed toward it.

The grass was still yellow. Even the evergreens had a lackluster color, blanched by the dry land-wind and the briny sea air. In this coastal park on the brink of twilight, at the end of winter rather than at the beginning of spring, there was not a soul to be seen.

Shozo walked up to the fence by the water's edge. In his ears was the roar of the waves beating against the steel pilings of the seawall. The blue-black water appeared cold, and only a distant portion of its surface reflected the dull golden light of evening. Floating upward against the western sky, tinged pale orange, was the city of Tokyo.

He had not gazed at the skyline for some time and was now astounded at how many more high-rises there were. Not long before, there had only been Tokyo Tower and the Tokyo World Trade Center Building, soaring in the foreground above the adjacent buildings of a mere ten stories or so, with the skyscrapers of Shinjuku appearing faintly in the background. Now lining both banks of the Sumida River as far as Shinagawa and Omori, there were many other buildings over twenty stories.

Some of these new high-rises had been built chockablock, while others were widely dispersed. There was no sense of coherence, as was only to be expected. Shozo's own company had been equally indifferent to the view of Tokyo as a whole when constructing office buildings and was likely to remain so. Neither the client nor the construction company could afford the luxury of such concern. In the struggle for survival, it was devour or be devoured.

Shozo understood it all very well but was nonetheless struck by the feeling that these buildings of steel and concrete had surreptitiously begun to multiply quite of their own volition. *Have we built a city or instead awakened and set loose an unknown power, an untamed species utterly different from the one that had, until now, grown fungal rows of slate-roof houses made of wood and paper? Something is in the process of ever-so-subtle transmutation. It is as though a force has begun to develop over which we human beings have already lost control.*

Suddenly, with a shrill whine from its engine, a white launch crossed in front of him, the waves from its wake thundering against the seawall. With hoarse cries, startled seagulls rose above his head and were gone. The wind had cooled. Shozo buttoned his jacket and turned up his collar.

I was quite unaware of it, but the children seem to have sensed the change taking place in the heart of Tokyo. So many of them could not possibly have come from just one or two groups, or even from three or four schools or districts. It's as though one night the children of Tokyo had all had the same dream and, one by one, mutely gathered.

The sky beyond the city presently shifted from reddish yellow to bright red and then to a deeper, more purplish color. The shadows of the crowded clutter of buildings grew still darker, and a desolate, ominous aura crept over all that Shozo could see before him. The ragged, blood-red clouds, driven by an untold wind, were scattering in sundry directions and with ever-changing shapes across the sky. It was as if across the entire western horizon, tongues of fire, fanned by that wind, were flickering behind the vast array of buildings.

So it had really burned! thought Shozo. It had been in the spring, about now, just before the end of the war. There had been massive air raids, night after night, from the area around the mouth of the Sumida River to Shinagawa and Omori. Had he been standing here then, he would have been engulfed in an inferno, emanating not only from the west but also from north and south. Every night it had been a virtual circle of fire, a fire that surely must have reached as far as the water's edge, set the sky ablaze, and illuminated the sea. Yet of that Shozo had no personal memory of his own, and so in his imagination he instead saw flames pouring out of every window of the Tokyo World Trade Center Building, Tokyo Tower collapsing in burning rubble, and, in the ferocious heat, all the countless new high-rises glowing and twisting. The fire was raging all around him. Even the rows of gas tanks behind Toyosu Wharf were bright red, sending up wave upon fiery wave.

Soon the conflagration had subsided, as the last flicker of evening light suddenly faded and a gray mist began to envelop the area. Even so, it was for Shozo as though he had indeed had a vision of portentous turbulence, descending on Tokyo and whirling through the streets like roaring flames.

He left the park, taking the exit nearest to the last bus stop. Directly from the rear of the gray dome where the children had gathered stretched a broad road, five lanes on each side, terminating where the park began.

Along the roadside, a few trucks and passenger cars had been left standing, but on the lanes themselves, as wide and flat as an airport runway, there was no sign of either vehicles or people. Though night had not yet fallen, the light of dusk was quite gone. The asphalt was a brownish, dry gray. To the left was the storage area for the cargo unloaded from the wharves; to the right, along the seawall, stood immense six- and seven-story warehouses. In the evening air of the artificial island, there was a raw chill.

Shozo sensed that all manner of things had been laid bare. As he began walking diagonally over the broad road toward the bus stop, he glanced fleetingly toward the top of the dome at the end of the vehicle lanes and thought to himself that the children would now be well on their way home. Suddenly from out of the shadow of that gray edifice he saw coming straight toward him a single, small, black dot, rending the tense stillness between day and night.

Though for a moment uncertain, he now recognized it as a motorcycle, approaching him at high speed, indeed at breakneck speed. Shozo, who was now standing close to the very middle, found himself forced to make an instant decision whether to move quickly forward or to retreat backward. He had no desire to run. As the road ended a dozen or so meters further on, the rider would have to slow down by the time he reached Shozo.

Shozo slightly quickened his pace, even as the motorcycle bore down on him with unrelenting velocity. He thought that by sheer momentum it would go plunging through the park, over the seawall, and into the water. He stood there frozen in the middle of the road. His paralysis was a reaction less to the apprehension of danger than to the sense of unreality.

It was a full-sized, high-performance machine. Despite its speed, the sound was no more than a low rumble as it came flying toward him. *He'll surely slow down or at least change his course*, thought Shozo. But now before he could cry out, the motorcycle had swept by, practically brushing the tip of his nose. The whoosh of air as it passed caused him to stagger.

He held his breath, fully expecting the rider to go crashing into the park fence. Yet with the front wheel having barely touched the enclosure, the machine came to a complete stop.

"Hey, you!" Shozo blurted out. "Isn't that a bit reckless?"

The youth turned the handlebars and rested one foot on the ground. For such a large machine, the rider seemed remarkably small. The figure's tight, black attire resembled a wetsuit, with half boots and helmet to match, the latter recalling the large, bulky headgear worn by underwater divers of a generation past, so that Shozo wondered whether it rendered inaudible any voices from the outside. The rider, black gloves resting on the handlebars, turned slowly to face him.

The visor was transparent, but the thicket inside the park cast a shadow, obscuring the cyclist's face. Suddenly all around them it was dark; only the silver metal of the motorcycle gave off a cold light.

The rider, apparently having stopped and turned about in surprise at seeing Shozo, gave no reply. Again he called out, this time in a louder voice, "You nearly knocked me over! You ought to keep your eye on the road!"

The youth slowly removed the black helmet. *What sort of person goes tearing along like a maniac and then is so silent? Clearly, some weird, frustrated, self-encapsulated kid.*

The seemingly heavy helmet came off with surprising ease. With two or three shakes of the rider's head, an abundance of long hair had fallen to her shoulders. Seeing that it was a woman, Shozo involuntarily caught his breath.

For a few moments both were silent. Shozo vaguely wondered how she had managed to keep her hair in the helmet. Had she twisted it up inside? Pinned it back? He had not seen her remove any sort of clasp.

The woman abruptly burst out laughing. "You're not going to be angry with a girl? You were glaring at me as though you were ready for a fight. Look, I simply didn't see you. I was entirely focused on just how far I could go full throttle and stop without crashing into the park."

"But that's so dangerous!"

"No. When I'm totally confident and concentrated on what's in front of me, the bike takes over. If you worry about what's just ahead or around you, you tighten up, and that's when you have an accident."

"But you were about to hit me."

"But I didn't now, did I? If I'd paid the slightest attention to you, I would definitely have crashed into either you or the fence."

Strange logic, he thought. Still, she had a frank way of speaking. An odd sort of person. There were a lot of young women in his company, and some of them were quite vivacious. But he had never met one like this before. He did not know whether what she was wearing was of leather or some synthetic material, but the firm yet pliable jet-black biker suit, the half boots, and the deerskin gloves seemed to suit her perfectly. And she was clearly in complete control of her huge, powerful, and efficient machine.

With one hand she held her helmet, while with the other she straightened her hair. She was perfectly calm. Though Shozo had never ridden a motorcycle, even he was capable of imagining what it was like—to be exposed to the wind and to danger, unprotected by the body of an ordinary car.

"In any case, you gave me quite a scare. And my heart's not back to normal."

"I'm very sorry. I'd offer to apologize by giving you a lift to wherever you're going, but the law says you've got to be wearing a helmet."

Shozo's response was immediate, as he shook his head, alarmed at the fleeting thought of racing along the bare asphalt clinging to the waist of this strange girl. "You must be joking. I'm not quite mad enough to want to perch myself behind a daredevil like you!"

The girl laughed and immediately switched on the motorcycle's stingingly powerful headlight. It illuminated the asphalt and the thicket in the park, the one reminding Shozo of a giant reptile's skin, the other of a crouching beast's thick, dark pelt.

"Well, there's not much I can do then. But at this hour you really shouldn't be loitering about in a place like this."

So saying, she abruptly donned her helmet, too fast for him to notice how she managed to enclose her long hair within it. She had hardly turned on the engine before swinging the machine around and driving off. The exhaust pipe flashed silver, as the bright headlight instantly and swiftly moved over the surface of the broad road. All at once she was gone. The dome roof too was now largely lost in the obscurity.

It had been neither a dream nor an illusion. He could still smell the gasoline. And yet it did not seem real. At the very least, there lingered a palpable sense of something quite alien to the world he had previously known and experienced. It was as though a black wind, full of an eerie life force, had suddenly passed through his body.

3

Shozo had begun going nearly every Sunday to the reclaimed land area. Advancing spring brought ever more people to the park and to the wharves, from which passenger ferries departed for Kyushu. Anglers, both young and old, had their lines in the water off the edge of the seawall. Couples with small children sat on the grass in the park, eating from packed lunch boxes. Especially on clear, windless afternoons, it was a soothing, heartwarming sight. On the ocean surface dots of light were dancing, and with every visit, even the call of the seagulls took on a certain charm. The flock of high-rises in the city beyond was obscured in the haze, allowing one to forget they were made of steel and concrete.

As he strolled among the people, Shozo watched the bobbing fishing lines and listened to the laughter of the toddlers on the grass. While this was quite pleasant and reassuring, it was at dusk as the crowd dwindled that he felt genuinely revived. It was then, with the rise of the wind, that the outlines of the high-rises beyond were again distinct and the artificial island's broad, straight road and rows of the warehouses began to reveal rough concrete and a nearly biting emptiness. The surface of the water and the asphalt shared the same sheen—blue-black and hard—that coldly deflected the gaze of all human eyes.

His visits had not necessarily been motivated by a desire for another meeting with the motorcycle rider. Yet when he stood alone in the dead silence of the twilight, he had the feeling that the black-clad figure on her immense silver machine might come suddenly from the far end of the road. He did not imagine her as coming either from Tsukiji over the Kachidoki Bridge and then through Tsukishima, or from Kiba in the old downtown area over the Toyosu and Harumi Bridges. It seemed more likely that she would issue forth from the opposite direction, from behind the gray, domed building through which the crowd of children had recently drifted. Though she was a bit older, it was as though she too had burst out onto the scene in full costume.

Since then, however, he had seen no such gathering, and the drab edifice was largely deserted and empty. Nor did the rider appear, despite Shozo's half-expectation. It was not because of her that he had made his way here, and yet each time he made his solitary way onto the bus, the darkness having deepened to the point that its yellow lights were shining brightly, he found himself feeling a keen disappointment, as though she had somehow failed to keep a rendezvous.

Once more taking out his map of the districts bordering To-kyo Bay, Shozo was astonished at the extent of the reclaimed land: it was much greater than he had imagined. Standing at Harumi Wharf and gazing over the water toward the city, he had the feeling of being in its center, but actually it only started there.

His work led him to assume that he knew the streets and neighborhoods of Tokyo, not only the positional relationships indicated on the map but also the precise elevation of the land, the hardness of the soil, and the drainage conditions. Yet the bay was for him a complete blind spot.

Allowing his eye to wander the entire map of the city, includ-ing the bay, he was surprised to see how deeply into the heart of the metropolis the water penetrated. The focal point, if judged from population distribution, would lie in the western region, beginning in Shinjuku, but when one looked solely at the old city, radiating out from the Imperial Palace and wedged between the two rivers—the Tamagawa in the west and the Arakawa in the east—nearly a quarter of the area was submerged. It seemed to Shozo as though land reclamation had advanced, quite beyond the reality of the capital's increasing refuse outflow, as though some immense and invisible force had suddenly begun filling in what the water had once gouged away.

A force working its will on Tokyo . . . Shozo had no truck with such "mysterious" or "spiritual" language or thinking; con-sciously, at least, it repelled him. And yet . . . When in his mind's eye he saw Tokyo's last forty years compressed into the space of mere minutes, as he looked out on the rows of barracks that had risen from the brown-red ashes assuming the outward form of domestic dwellings, filling the old city in the twinkling of an eye, and now moving slowly but inexorably into the suburbs, even as in the urban center high-rises were sprouting up with expressways and subways ringing the city, it was as though a single, seething, subterranean mass of slime mold had been formed from an infinite number of microorganisms and was now projecting its crowned stalks skyward. In this, he sensed a power quite beyond his understanding.

It was the power of Nature itself, containing within it the unconscious, the inorganic. Shozo had quite consciously taken part in the transformation of Tokyo, but now he felt a force that utterly dwarfed his tiny self.

No, that was not it. He too was part of that force. It had worked through and in him; it continued to do so, stirring his inner being. The vague sensation altered his self-awareness, as though he were someone quite distinct from the person he had previously thought himself to have been. He was still that person and yet in some sense another, an unknown other. It occurred to him that the same power that was driving Tokyo to fill in the land that the bay had torn away was clearly beckoning him here. It gave him an eerie, yet invigorating feeling.

Looking at the map, Shozo discovered a bus route running from the Shinagawa area to Koto Ward, traversing the area of reclaimed land. One Sunday afternoon, despite an overcast sky and the imminent threat of rain, he jauntily set out from home.

He took a taxi as far as Shinagawa. Then, unable to find the bus stop, he asked several people—in a strangely low and timid voice. It was not that he was inquiring about a disreputable neighborhood. Perhaps he was embarrassed by an impulsiveness inappropriate to his years. And yet what, he wondered, could be wrong with following the urgings of one's own heart? He had no answer to that.

The bus stop was located on the corner of a bare and dirty lot. Two girls of high-school age were waiting there. The bus, one of the older models, soon arrived. Just as the doors were closing, several men barged aboard and, taking seats on either side of the aisle, began talking about horse racing.

The bus had smoothly set off and was now passing through an industrial area. There was a monotonous procession of long walls and warehouses, as gray as the low-hanging clouds. With the unrestrained volume of the men's chatter and their deliberately raucous laughter, Shozo seemed to have entered a world quite distinct from the urban center's subway lines on which he daily traveled. Along the avenue there were scarcely any pedestrians. The rows of warehouses were dark and forlorn; on the bank of a black and stagnant canal an old and rotting boat was moored. As they passed under the expressway, he could clearly see cracks and stains in the concrete supports.

They crossed a bridge and entered the reclaimed land area. Above a newly completed high-rise apartment complex, Shozo saw the body of a jetliner coming in to land at Haneda Airport, though the sound of the engines was inaudible to him. The men who had been returning from the racetrack had already gotten off, and other than the girls sitting silently next to each other in a corner, he was the only remaining passenger.

The bus had now entered a broad thoroughfare, busy with trucks even on a Sunday. This, he knew, was the Bayshore Route, but as they passed through the tunnel with its reddish-yellow illumination, he could hardly believe that they were really under water. Tokyo's tentacles extended even to the ocean bottom. The areas of Tsukishima and Harumi already resembled land, with their seawater lakes and giant canals.

As they emerged from the tunnel, the bus left the expressway and turned into a wide avenue, thick on both sides with trees and weedy undergrowth. The whitish soil had obviously been transported from another location, but otherwise the artificial island was hardly different from inland suburban housing developments built on leveled land.

Directly in front of them was the Museum of Maritime Science, a steamer-shaped concrete edifice. Beyond a short bridge nearby lay a broad expanse of land. It seemed truly immense, for the straight road stretching before them went on and on. With no bordering trees, it was all a vast field of weeds, still dominated by the withered, yellowish brown of winter. *There indeed*, he thought, his heart pounding, *lies the reclaimed land*.

The bus was about to turn toward the museum. Seeing an upcoming stop, Shozo gave an impulsive push to the stop button and got off. Whichever way he looked, there was not another human figure in sight. A ditchlike waterway was filled with dull, leaden water.

He was alone as he crossed the bridge. The low, static clouds and the broad asphalt under his feet were of the same color. As he reached the reclaimed land, he saw that the road and the field were even more desolately vast than they had appeared from the windows of the bus. Looming out of the emptiness as an immense, white specter was the museum. The outlines of the Tokyo high-rises had been dissolved behind the gray clouds. The giant gantry cranes on the Oi Pier appeared as a row of skeletal giraffes that had perished as they stood against the chimerical horizon.

Only recently had he experienced how the broad, deserted stretch of asphalt along the Harumi Wharf could chafe at the skin of the soul, but there the scent of the city had wafted in across the surface of the narrow stretch of water. It had been as though, depending on the wind, one might hear the hubbub of the city.

Where he now stood was a true wilderness, but one with neither the smell of millennia nor the gravity of earth. Had it been ten years since the construction of this artificial land? Twenty?

Shozo left the street and wandered into the field. There was a thicket of reed-like grass, hard and withered, growing higher than his head, then completely barren, cracked ground, from which protruded wires, plastic bags, and a piece of reddish kimono material. Though covered with dirt, none of this refuse, including tools and other bits of clothing, appeared the least decayed. Indeed, there was something starkly vivid about it. He was startled to find kindled in him a feeling bordering on the sexual, something which, since the death of his wife, he had thought irrelevant to him.

His work took him with some frequency to clubs in the Ginza, but he had long since ceased to experience any sexual arousal, even when a young and sensuous hostess was snuggled next to him or when he strolled through an entertainment district with its provocative neon lights and advertisements. Why here, at the edge of this completely deserted patch of reclaimed land . . . ? A mere scrap of clothing poking out of the ground had filled him with far more lascivious thoughts than might a naked female body. And this was only intensified as he contemplated the pale, dry, inorganic soil.

Shozo had never fallen head over heels in love. As a student, still amid the ruins of the postwar years, university classes and his part-time work had given him more than enough to do. His supervisor had acted as the guiding hand in his entirely conventional arranged marriage, and he had stayed away from bargirls and prostitutes out of fear of disease. As he idly wandered about the field, it occurred to him that while he had not been particularly interested in making a career for himself, he had, in fact, remained tied to his job.

The open land that from the road had appeared quite flat proved to be rather hilly. Natural subsidence, it would seem, occurred according to the quality of refuse used as landfill. With the irregularity of the terrain, Shozo could not find his way to the end of the field, though he trudged on and on. The tall, withered grass cut off his vision; perhaps he was just going in circles. Yet in the unexpected sense of liberation that this ramble over the barren artificial land had given him, he found an intense, even achingly intense, pleasure.

It might have been a different kind of pleasure had there been sunshine or an agreeable breeze. Under the low, thick clouds that bore down on him in the windless, oppressive stillness, he retreated to his inner feelings, reinforced by the bleak surroundings.

Shozo's travels had always been restricted to company matters. Once in his mid-thirties, however, he had, on his return from a business trip to Kyoto, been abruptly seized by a desire to visit the tip of Noto Peninsula. He went to Kanazawa and from there on to Wajima. The town was not what he had expected, and so, disappointed, he had set off again to return to Kanazawa. As the train came to a small station, whose name he did not even know, he thought that he heard the sound of the ocean and, on a whim, got off. It was late autumn and already dark. Except for a small travel bag he had no luggage, and so he immediately left the station and walked through the streets as though possessed, following the roar of the waves and the smell of the sea.

He groped his way along a path that led through a pinewood, until suddenly the ocean lay before him. On the beach it was all he could do to remain standing against the spray, the strong wind, and the swirling sand, but there alone on that stormy beach on a pre-winter evening, he felt surging from within his chilled body an alien, savage force . . . It exuded something astonishingly strong, sexual, and violent. Breathing heavily, he brooded that if on the path back to town he were to encounter a woman, young or old, he would instantly throw her to the ground. Fortunately, no woman in such a provincial community would have been out walking alone at night. Now, some twenty years later, he was recalling the nearly forgotten memory of that extraordinary emotion.

There on the seashore in an utterly strange locality, at the outer edge of solitude, alone in a world of black waves, wind, darkness, and whipping sand, he had abruptly experienced the sensation of no longer being himself, of being held in the grip of another . . . Indeed, as never before, he had experienced himself as a strange monstrosity, a soft, hot, wriggling mass, with thrashing, invisible tentacles. In that inexplicable organism, which would never be captured in any mirror or photograph, he had seen his true self. This ego of his (Shozo glanced down at himself, at his arms, body, trousers, and dirty shoes) was nothing but an unseemly projection into the three-dimensional world.

Shozo abruptly raised his head, detecting a slow-moving object close at hand. Stretching out all about him was withered grass, taller than himself. Within it there now appeared an immense, dark, silently creeping shadow, filling his field of vision.

With bated breath he followed the phantom. After a few moments he recognized it as a ship, a monstrously large ship with a rusted stern. There was scarcely a spot on the vessel that was not peeling paint. The cabins and smokestacks were all far to the rear, as though having been perfunctorily placed there. Yet how was it that a large sea vessel had made its way into this thicket? Until just a few moments before, he had seen nothing.

It seemed to him, if not a complete hallucination, at least a mirage. Pushing through the thick grass, he made his way toward the huge, looming shadow of the ship. Though uncomprehending, he did not think it in any way unnatural. He had the strong feeling that here one should be prepared for anything. He experienced a sense of dizziness, rather more akin to euphoria.

As he struggled to orientate himself by looking in vain for something higher than the withered grass, his gaze fixed above him, he might well have fallen into the water, for now he had come to the end of the reclaimed land. A freighter was slowly moving over the surface in front of him, and as it gradually disappeared into the distance, all became at last clear to him, though the intensely real but uncanny feeling remained that a black ship had, in fact, silently glided by through the reeds. The freighter there on the leaden sea appeared more illusory, as did the jet passenger planes that one after another were coming in to land at Haneda.

4

Shozo had sensed that on Sundays he became a different person. Now he felt that it was during his wanderings about the reclaimed land that he was his true self, while during the week he was someone else.

This is not to say that he in any way neglected his work from Monday to Friday. He devoted his other free time, on alternate Saturdays, to cleaning, shopping, and other household duties; in the evening, he would relax in a completely neutral frame of mind in front of the television.

After a downturn, his company's profits were again slowly rising. Having never been ruthlessly bent on a career, Shozo belonged to no faction and likewise had no particular enemies. He was not a go-getter but was nonetheless conscientious and earnest, and even if he did keep his true thoughts to himself, he was not regarded as reclusive.

He continued to go drinking with customers and colleagues several times a week. In fact, people even said that his appearance had become more youthful. "Usually," someone would say, "a woman widowed after middle age picks up vim, while widowers go to seed. He must've found himself someone new, a de facto wife." But this invariably brought a rejoinder: "Not Sakai. He's in love with high-rises. On his days off, he goes around looking at buildings."

That was certainly not so far off the mark. True, Shozo no longer spent his Sundays ambling about urban edifices, but when his work took him out on errands he would still stop to look at unusual constructions or new buildings. Increasingly, there were innovative projects being designed by young architects. Despite what was no doubt fierce competition, they were, it seemed to him, carrying out their endeavors with bold determination. It was a pleasure to see the fruits of their labors.

It was on just such a day that, having finished his remaining work in the office, he left for home at a little after nine. Hurrying to the subway through the dark, still streets that belied the daylight pedestrian traffic, he found himself stopping unexpectedly to gaze at a show window that was just then being decorated.

It was one of those stylish shops for clothing, personal adornment, designer furniture, and decorative objects that had begun to spring up, one after another, in the business districts. In this hushed, nocturnal street, where otherwise only the street lamps were illuminated, the brightly lit show window offered a miniature panorama. Yet it was not merely the lighting that suddenly and powerfully drew his attention. Several men were hammering the last nails in the wall and cleaning up debris from the floor, but their work was nearly complete and it was this, the decorative setting, that caught him by surprise and made a deep impression on his mind.

It was a scene with mannequins, but not of the strangely smooth, featureless variety that had recently become fashionable. Even in their expressions, as well as in their faces, hair, and limbs, these appeared indistinguishable from human beings. A small family of them was sitting in a Western-style living room. The figures were dressed in unobtrusive, ordinary domestic wear, but the color scheme and design had been so skillfully arranged as to suggest expensive imports.

Though the room was smaller than in real life, the casually laid out furniture, daily necessities, and ornaments were all genuine. On the walls and the floor there were even hints of stains and cracks. Neither the implements nor the décor as a whole came from the present but rather suggested the tasteful simplicity of a time gone by. Here in panorama was an interior view of a prewar Western-style house, such as could still be seen in the older quarters of the city. Yet a closer look revealed something more than the quaint and nostalgic.

The bodily orientation of the middle-aged couple, the grandfather, and the young daughter and the direction toward which their eyes pointed were at complete variance. The old man, seated in an easy chair with a book open on his lap, was staring up at a corner of the ceiling. The husband and wife sat across from each other at the tea table, but they were looking past each other, so that there was something distinctly eerie about their beaming faces. The daughter was gazing into a gilt-edged mirror hanging on the wall above a shelf inlaid with mother-of-pearl, but through some trick this reflected a face other than her own. Her hair was bound, and she wore only light cosmetics, while her counterpart was tousle-haired, with heavily made-up eyelids and a flaming red mouth that was gaping in a laugh.

Moreover a boy, apparently the younger brother of the girl, was preparing to jump out of the room through a wide-open window. With his head raised and his limbs aligned and extended, as though he were about to dive into a swimming pool, he seemed on the verge of leaping over the dense, strangely shaped tropical garden plants into the violet night sky, in which a full moon was shining.

The members of the family were all on their own, their invisible bonds broken, their postures, facial expressions, and gazes frozen. The ice-cold stillness so characteristic of mannequins reigned over the entire room. And as this stillness was self-generating, it harmonized superbly with the silence of the room's ornate furniture and household accessories. As if that were not enough, it was all dissolved in the ambience of the dark and deserted business district—the thick display window, the concrete walls, the empty pavement, and the rows of now unilluminated windows.

By the light of day, he thought, with the bustling crowds and the din of the street, it might be seen as nothing more than an obvious artifact. At this moment, however, the small panorama had quite engulfed and penetrated the nighttime scene of urban concrete and, with it, Shozo's own mind. The deep stillness was eerie and at the same time evoked in him a vague sense of nostalgia. He shuddered, even as he felt pleasantly drawn to it. What sort of person had devised such a setting?

The men had at some point vanished. Alone in the middle of the room stood a woman, gently shifting the mannequins and adjusting their clothing. As her back was turned to him, he could not see her face. Tall and slender, she wore a windbreaker and pantaloon-like trousers of olive green, baggy at the hips but narrowing at the ankles.

For some time, she remained nearly motionless, occasionally turning her head ever so slightly to concentrate her gaze on what seemed most likely to be her own work. Yet she did not conform to the image he might have had of a woman in such an occupation; there was no suggestion that she was self-consciously putting on a gaudy, exuberant show. She appeared so subdued that one might have thought that she herself was one of her own mannequins.

Shozo gradually found himself to be less interested in the setting than in its apparent creator. He did not know to what extent the work reflected the intentions of those who had commissioned it, as opposed to the plan of the designer, but he clearly sensed that what had been sought was not merely a display of eccentricity for the sake of drawing the customer's attention. Here was revealed something profound, though in the realm of neither ideas nor art: a compellingly realistic and personal vision. Perhaps there was something even deeper, of which she herself was unaware. What sort of woman was this, who was unconsciously experiencing such feelings?

At that moment, half of the bright illumination in the room was extinguished. From out of the shadows appeared the face of a man, who spoke to the woman. She replied, then looked slowly around the entire set as though for final verification. In so doing, she caught sight of Shozo standing in the street on the other side of the window. She showed no sign of being startled.

She was much younger than he had supposed, having seen her only from the back. Her sharply chiseled face, with only a few traces of makeup, was terribly pale. She gave the impression of being so sensitive and keenly observant as to be struggling to avoid collapse.

Their eyes met, hers narrowing, as she stared at him; they were not disapproving but nonetheless severe. Subtly attempting to intercept her sharp gaze, he offered a weak smile, then nodded several times, pointing with one hand to the display in the show window.

Her frown appeared to dissipate ever so slightly, but her expression remained hard. Then she turned and left the room.

The lights were now all extinguished. Yet the mannequins remained sitting, smiling as before, one continuing to stare into the mirror, another about to jump into the evening sky.

The lights were still burning in the restaurant district in front of the station. Even now there remained vividly in his mind the image of the young woman as one of her own mannequins, standing up and turning around to face him.

5

Shozo was increasingly aware that something within him was beginning to change. He did not know why, nor was he himself seeking change. If the cause was, so to speak, the experience of bachelorhood *d'après saison*, the death of his wife having come after his prime, the alteration would surely have been set in motion much earlier. Yet, in fact, his daily routine had remained much as it had been before. He continued to reside in the same apartment, to commute to the same company, to eat the same food, and to wear the same clothes. Being childless, he and his wife had dined out several times a week. Moreover, having long been single—first, of course, as a student and later as a company employee—he had been accustomed to cooking for himself, for in those days there had not yet been the restaurants and pubs where one could now enjoy simple and tasty dishes. Even after his marriage, when he was already over thirty, he had often taken his turn in the kitchen.

On losing his wife, he had received genuinely sympathetic words to the effect that life without her would surely cause him day-to-day difficulties. Yet though he experienced loneliness, he felt no such inconvenience.

It occurred to him that the sudden transformation had been initiated by his encounter with the strange children in Harumi on the reclaimed land. And the result was not merely his trips to Tokyo Bay on his days off. He began to wear dress shirts that were other than white—still light in color, but beige, sky blue, or striped. He had also added a few new, bright neckties to his wardrobe. A large supermarket with many imported items had opened nearby, and there he began to purchase unusually oily foods: snails, assorted varieties of cheese, beef tongue, and lamb.

He had started to dream more frequently, too. This may have been partly due to the greater inclination at his age to awaken at dawn. When he got out of bed and sat on the living-room sofa, he could see through the window the street lamps below, flickering several times before going out, one after the other. In the faint half-light between night and morning, his reveries of a few minutes before appeared to him, as though he were slowly rewinding and replaying a videocassette.

He finds himself, for example, in an old, dilapidated wooden house. A small plastic model airplane, a fighter from a World War II American warship, comes careening in and crashes into the rotting wall planks, lodging itself there before bursting into reddish yellow flames that slowly spread from the planks to the ceiling . . . The color of those quivering flames would then float up into the air above the dim, empty street below.

In such moments when the pale light shone through the window, the small items lying strewn over the table—his lighter, magnifying glass, and key holder—assumed a strange lightness and extraordinary beauty, neither illusory nor real.

Shozo had still been a middle-school boy in the last days of the war. Despite a widespread conviction that a "divine wind" would alter the course of the war and give victory to Japan, in the end not even a puff had blown. Ever since, he had rejected with a sense of abhorrence any suggestion of the supernatural, not only mere superstition but bona fide religion as well. He had come to realize that, even if he did not fully understand it, the ongoing attachment he felt for the angular high-rises, with their precisely intersecting lines, arose at least in part from his dislike of uncertainty and ambiguity.

He thus found it odd that he had taken recent coincidences perfectly in his stride, not considering them in the least absurd. This state of mind remained unaltered when at work he received a telephone call from a school chum working in the Ports and Harbors Bureau of the metropolitan government.

The purpose of the call was only to inform him of a class reunion, but as Shozo had not spoken to him in some time and for all of his frequent outings to Tokyo Bay had not once remembered that he had a friend in the bureau, he had the visceral sense that someone had summoned the man.

They had been talking about a mutual acquaintance, when Shozo surprised the other with a question: "Where in Tokyo Bay is refuse being disposed of?"

"Why would that interest you? Does it involve a construction project?"

"No, just personal curiosity."

Amused that Shozo would concern himself with refuse, his friend laughed and then replied, "It's beyond Reclaimed Land Site #13; the place is officially known as the outer section of the Central Breakwater Reclaimed Land Site."

"Reclaimed Land Site #13?"

"Yes, just past the Museum of Maritime Science."

"You mean that huge area of land? I recently took the bus there one Sunday."

"I'm amazed. Since when have you gone prowling about such a place?"

"It's something quite new. I feel drawn to it, though I myself don't know why. Perhaps one reason is that it reminds me of the burned-out ruins of our childhood. It's just that it's wistfully familiar, as though I were taking a journey home."

"War ruins? Nowadays?"

"I know it's absurd. But recently I've had the strange feeling that I need to verify some sort of starting point. We've been working like madmen for thirty years. Who *are* we, and what have we been doing?"

"You're showing your age."

"Perhaps. But I don't think I'm merely reminiscing. We've been cramming buildings onto narrow strips where every cubic foot is worth its weight in gold. So the sight of such vast, empty space is quite moving. The very idea of man-made land makes one imagine what sort of habitations might be built there. There's something hallucinatory about it, quite contrary to my nature. Well, no, I suppose that's not the right word for it. To put it simply, it's as though I were in a different world, a kind of desert, although I've never actually been to one. I feel that I become a different person there."

Much to his own astonishment, Shozo spoke with unguarded exuberance.

"I see. Well then, how would it be if I took you there?"

"No, I like rambling about on my own. Is it possible to go where they're dumping the refuse?"

"No, it's off-limits."

"All right, in that case, I suppose I'll ask for your help."

"Actually, it's the Sanitation Bureau that handles refuse. But I'll speak to those in charge."

As they talked, Shozo could feel the force of some unknown person or will driving him to that place. He was surprised at his own thoughts.

On a clear Saturday afternoon Shozo rode a taxi all along the road through Reclaimed Land Site #13 and got out at the entrance to the seabed tunnel leading to the inner section of the Central Breakwater Reclaimed Land Site. There was a huge ventilation tower, identical to the one at the Bayshore Route's seabed tunnel through which he came whenever he took the bus from Shinagawa.

As arranged, an official dressed in work clothes and a yellow helmet picked up Shozo in a jeep and took him back into the same tunnel from which he had emerged. Blue garbage trucks passed them as they went. Though the center of the capital was a mere stone's throw away, Shozo felt excited, as though he were being taken to a distant terra incognita.

Ordinary raw household garbage, the official explained, was currently being incinerated at the various ward disposal sites and the ashes then delivered to them. Only nonburnable and oversized refuse came directly here.

As they emerged from the tunnel, a small mountain of coarse earth rose to their left. "Is that all refuse?" Shozo asked incredulously, to which the official replied serenely, "The refuse and soil are sandwiched together in layers. They make for quite a pile now, but they subside over time."

"On their own?"

"Yes, on their own."

The pile was immense. On its flat summit, bulldozers were leveling out the refuse. Vent-like pipes protruded here and there. "They serve to release the accumulated methane gas. It's quite a hazard, so please don't smoke here."

Above some areas that appeared to have been already leveled was a swarm of seagulls along with a few crows, the sun catching on the black and white feathers. It was only when humans were immediately upon them that the remarkably portly seagulls took flight.

Far beyond the broad expanse of newly created land with its wharfs and gas tanks, and the sea glittering in the sun, were the smog-veiled high-rises of the urban center.

The mountain of refuse that Tokyo spewed forth was creating the land for the Tokyo of the future. It struck Shozo as a circular flow, an immense yet invisible cycle—devised, planned, and carried out by humans, to be sure, but nonetheless driven by a mightier power behind it all. The stench of rot hung in the air, blending with the smell of the sea. Within the mounds, methane gas was bubbling and gurgling up. The ground on which he stood was even at that moment slowly sinking. He could feel the wriggling movement, the breath, the body temperature of Tokyo, as it ceaselessly filled the vacuum of the bay.

They drove in the jeep as far as the outer section of the Central Breakwater Reclaimed Land Site, where the landfill project had first been launched. Concrete walls surrounded a vast area of seawater, larger than the whole of Tsukishima. This was where refuse was being dumped.

Most of what lay floating on the water's surface was wrapped in white plastic bags. Shozo had not imagined that plastic bags could sparkle with such brilliance in the sunlight. Though obviously dirty, they reflected the direct rays, as though covered with silver leaf or aluminum dust. Mixed in were many blue and a few black bags. Shozo thought he had never seen anything so spectacular. How could a refuse dump, he wondered incredulously, be capable of displaying such beauty?

From the edge of the access road on the cement wall, he looked down on the mountainous heaps of floating bags. Protruding from them were all sorts of objects: a purse with a torn strap; a worn and rusted wire net for grilling fish; a nude photograph from a weekly magazine; a bundle of discarded fliers for the previous spring labor offensive, included in the nonburnable refuse despite not belonging there; an alarm clock without hands; torn pantyhose; a black-bound office notebook; a bundle of spaghetti; a child's red sports shoe.

Every item of rubbish, broken and tossed aside, exuded an intense sense of being, a pungent odor of life. On the shelf of a shop or a department store, they would have appeared quite ordinary, drawing not the least emotion. Yet now they gleamed like precious ore just unearthed, each asserting itself, each telling its own story. The wire net easily evoked a kitchen, the smoke of roasting mackerel, and the faces of a family around the dinner table. The alarm clock embodied the grogginess of the early morning, freezing water in a washbasin, and the scene of a packed commuter train. The single red shoe gave a picture of a smiling girl whose mother had bought the pair, the concrete floor of a vestibule, and rope skipping in the nearby alleys.

Shozo was quite unprepared for the almost choking feeling that came upon him. Broken, separated, fragmented, and discarded, these objects had gained new life. Looking out over the mass of scattered refuse, one might well take it for a sign of the power of entropy. They had not been reduced to nothingness, to a state of atrophy; instead, they exuded something rich, viscous, and potent. Exposed here were the normally hidden entrails of ever-urbanizing, ever-soaring Tokyo, its streets emptying of people and its air growing thinner.

"Are you all right?" the official asked worriedly, noting that Shozo had been staring for some time in silence at the refuse.

"Yes, I'm fine," he replied, and then stammered, "It's just that I don't understand why it all seems so very much alive."

The official laughed, holding his hand over his eyes to shield them from the bright light of the sun. "I wonder how much longer it will take before this is filled? We're almost at that point now. How will we be able to dispose of it all after that?"

This seemed indeed to be the crux of the matter. Tokyo was expanding (vertically, having already reached its horizontal limits), brimming over with commodities (devoid of either the light or the shadow of history), the ever-increasing refuse (with many items unnecessarily discarded) brought to life again between the water and the light (with the glittering plastic bags and the wheezing cacophony of garbage).

Yet more and more was covered with soil, bulldozed level, then allowed to settle, dissolve, and decay, until land came into being. Thus, Tokyo continued to spread.

And the flood of commodities too went on, along with increasing numbers of them being discarded. They too would gleam for a moment with new life before likewise sinking, dissolving, and decaying.

Tokyo lives, thought Shozo. No, he pondered further, as he recalled the view he had just seen of the distant, smog-enshrouded city from atop the mound of refuse, "Tokyo" is only what we call a quivering, breathing, expanding presence, a shape maintained by the endless belching forth of waste, exhaust, sewer water, heat, radio waves, noise, and idle chatter; a circulatory mechanism, invisible but powerful, created and controlled by no one. Panting and trembling, growing and cracking, the ice-cold high-rises and the solid elevated highways have all been born and bred within that system.

Just as when one experiences severe diarrhea the bowels seem to move of their own accord, Shozo felt that everything in and around him was slowly and ominously stirring. At the same time, he was aware of how he was gradually twisting in on himself. *And when I have been twisted to the breaking point and cast upon the rubbish heap, will I too acquire light and shadow and then begin to tell my story?*

"We have another facility for the disposal of oversized refuse. Would you care to see it?"

Shozo was already quite fatigued, but in order not to appear unappreciative of the official's hospitality he replied simply, "Yes, thank you."

The installation resembled a small silo in which large refuse items such as sofas, refrigerators, and beds were being taken up by a conveyor belt to a rotating shaft in the turret and there crushed. They went inside. In the control room, monitors indicated the status of the operation; the extra-large objects, for all their seeming solidity, were being splendidly smashed and pulverized.

Shozo gazed absentmindedly at the monitor screens and then gasped in surprise. In the midst of the swirling dust and splinters in the obscurity of the disintegration turret, a head was floating upward and now dominated the entire picture. Shozo immediately saw that it was from a mannequin. Though the image appeared for only a moment, the severed head, hairless and smooth, of an unmistakably female figure, of which only the lips shone bright red, was all the more vivid for having not the slightest scratch upon its face.

It was not because it might have been taken for a human head. It was clearly a mannequin—yet nonetheless alive. Something that ought to be lifeless seemed to be living. He was seized by the bizarre feeling that what had rightly been a clear and distinct boundary had abruptly vanished. All the more bizarre was the ambrosial sense of giddiness that accompanied it.

The emotion was known to him. A memory he thought he had lost—of the oddly lifelike set of show-window mannequins on that evening in the business district and the strange young woman who had created it—came back to him in full force.

It occurred to him that the woman had been treating mannequins as human and thus regarded humans as mannequins—perhaps above all herself.

The thought gave him a sense of commonality with her. Perhaps the woman and he—still fascinated by high-rises—were kindred spirits. If that was abnormal, then they shared the same illness.

"Does that happen often?" asked Shozo, as they returned to the jeep.

"What do you mean?"

"The head of the mannequin that was being taken up on the conveyor belt to be crushed . . ."

"Was there such a thing?" the official asked dubiously. "I didn't see it."

As they emerged from the seabed tunnel, the sun was just beginning to tinge Reclaimed Land Site #13 in evening light. Shozo courteously took his leave from the official and walked to the bus stop near the Museum of Maritime Science. The straight and empty street had turned dark red. He was physically fatigued but emotionally aroused.

Ranging to his left was the field of weeds that he had recently wandered over, and where he had seen protruding from the parched earth the ends of wires and the edge of a woman's kimono. Now he understood how this broad expanse of land had been created—and what was tightly packed and buried beneath, layer upon layer.

All manner of objects, each steeped in its own history, lay piled on one another, ten, no, fifteen meters below. Wild and overgrown, the entire plain seemed to be breathing deeply. The asphalt of the deserted street was gently rolling.

From the heart of his being, Shozo dimly felt a surge of vital energy. The buildings of Tokyo silhouetted against the evening sky now struck him as terribly distant.

6

This evening, too, the sunset on the reclaimed land was beautiful, particularly here on Site #13, devoid of buildings other
than a row of level warehouses along the eastern bank. On the
southern edge where he had recently been, the lone ventilation
tower of the seabed tunnel soared into the sky, but this was still
the most extensive and the emptiest area and would remain so
until the inner and outer sections of the Central Breakwater Reclaimed Land Site were filled in.

The westering sun was unblocked by any edifice. A weak blue
evening haze had descended over the entire plain, which then
abruptly turned to deep green, and in the dying light shifted
entirely to a pale red, then to a dreamlike violet.

Shozo sat down on the edge of a grassy knoll and gazed at a
group of motorcyclists racing along the broad road that stretched

in a straight line some fifty meters before him. As they passed, their engines momentarily made a deafening roar that, unimpeded by any reverberating object, quickly disseminated into the air and was muffled in the haze.

The gang numbered a dozen or so. They appeared to be engaged in competition on the empty street; all were riding large and powerful machines. When a group of them went by, he could feel the ground shaking. They drove at high speed, well over a hundred kilometers per hour.

As soon as they had appeared, Shozo had eagerly looked to see whether the biker he had met in Harumi was among them, but the riders all looked the same in their identical clothing and large helmets, so much so that one could not even distinguish male from female. She had driven very fast, to be sure, but not at this insane velocity. No woman, however skillful, would drive so heedlessly. Moreover, he sensed that she was hardly one to join such a delinquent gang.

So she was not there, he concluded with mild disappointment. At the same time, he was gradually coming to understand that these young people, driving their motorcycles at full force, were experiencing the intimate feel of the open air in a way that no automobile could provide. No doubt this was the only such pure space in the entire Tokyo area. Were there moments in which they felt themselves at one with it, sensing that it was not simply empty but had a pliancy and elasticity emanating from some hidden force within . . . ?

Still, however wide the road, their manner of riding was dangerous. With a dozen of them roaring along in a pack, they needed to do nothing more than graze or bump another to become a heap of twisted scrap.

There was an air of unreality about them. They appeared suddenly like a black wind blowing across the field, only to turn and vanish back into the same violet evening haze. The feeling was intensified with the thickening of the mist. Shozo marveled at how they were able to go on endlessly repeating the same pattern, following the same course, to and fro.

Thus lost in thought, Shozo was at first unaware that the riders, in almost a parade formation just beyond his gaze, had abruptly been thrown into disarray, with two at one end sent flying as though flicked from the road like marbles. In stark slow motion, they arced through the air, machine and rider, and landed in the grass. Shozo gave a shout and jumped up, though feeling somehow that it was not he himself reacting.

One of the motorcycles lay fairly close to the road, the other at some distance into the field. Having rolled over two or three times, the rider of the latter stood up again with surprisingly little effort, righted his fallen cycle, remounted it, and drove back across the grass to the road in pursuit of his companions, who had now disappeared.

"How strange," thought Shozo in disbelief, as he stood rooted to the spot. "Can the others simply drive away? Surely they'll come right back!" But the roar of the engines faded away, with no sign of their return.

Shozo stayed where he was, having assumed that if the one rider had recovered so easily, the other, who had flown the shorter distance, would not be seriously injured. But the biker, lying face down, the engine of the toppled machine still humming, did not get up. Nonetheless convinced that, with the realization that one of their numbers was missing, the others would soon be back, Shozo remained motionless.

Yet they did *not* return, and the idling engine continued to splutter. On the stainless steel of the handlebars, pointed skywards, the reflection of the evening sun flickered.

"What are they doing?" grumbled Shozo, as he slowly moved closer. The rider lay still. "Oh, no, he can't be dead!" he thought. There was no sign of blood.

"Hey, are you all right?" he called out, but there was no reaction. He nudged the figure in the back. The material of the clothing was thick, but soft to the touch.

"Ah! Could it be *her*?" The nightmarish thought flashed suddenly across his mind. "It's all because of this reckless behavior." He was uncontrollably vexed. Here he had been basking pleasantly in the twilight, and now this had abruptly landed on him.

Shozo turned the rider over, seizing the shoulders as though with deliberate force. He detected what seemed to be a weak moan. There was a swelling of the chest. He looked through the helmet's visor but could not make out the face. Taking off one of the leather gloves, he touched a slender female wrist. Her pulse was beating. Once again he surveyed her entire body. She had undoubtedly been injured, but there was no external bleeding.

He shook her shoulders and tapped sharply on her visor, but she remained unconscious. She must have struck her head hard against the ground, but Shozo had no way of knowing whether, even with her thick helmet, that might be a serious matter.

Again he shook her by the shoulders, which moved limply in his grip. He peered down the road, but there was no sign of either automobiles or people, to say nothing of the girl's companions. There was only the haze deepening rapidly from violet to indigo. Shozo turned off the engine. Instantly, a stillness fell, blending with the smell of the brine. He had the distinct feeling of being alone at the bottom of a deep body of water with the remains of a drowned woman.

Aware that he must quickly come up with a plan of action, he felt at the same time a strong desire simply to remain there. Though there was hardly any light, the motorcycle's chrome components still gleamed splendidly. Encased in a black windbreaker, the girl's chest softly rose and fell. He could see less and less through the visor, but from what he could see, she did not seem to be in pain as she lay there, totally defenseless. Whether it was foolishness or audacity, to be racing at such speeds in such a pack was only to invite this sort of accident.

It was all too difficult for Shozo to comprehend, but that only piqued his curiosity, as though he had before him a biological entity previously unknown and quite uncanny.

For a third time, he put his hands on her shoulders and shook her. There was no reaction. Through the thick fabric, her limp body felt like that of an invertebrate. With his hands still on her shoulders, he had in immediate view the zipper of her jacket. Were he now to open it ever so gently and unbutton the blouse beneath it, what sort of flesh would emerge?

He remembered his conversation with the official at the refuse disposal site.

"Does it *all* rot and dissolve?"

"Yes, eventually."

"But plastic doesn't rot, does it?"

"Plastic disintegrates too."

"I had thought it didn't."

"It does. When other substances rot, they emit heat."

What am I thinking? He found his fingers fumbling for the zipper tab.

He took a deep breath and got up. He felt a choking sensation and, at the same time, a throbbing within him that he had never known before. For several moments, he stared at the woman with her outstretched arms and legs, wrapped tightly in black. There was no one there to see him.

A wind-like force suddenly blew through his body. In the end, he thought, everything rots.

The vivid image that had been carried directly from beneath his feet—of layers of refuse ten or fifteen meters thick, sinking and rotting—now faded away.

He walked back to the road and then toward the Bayshore Route. The only vehicles driving past were trucks, but surely a taxi would come along sooner or later.

By the time Shozo was able to catch a cab and return, Reclaimed Land Site #13 was engulfed in viscidly thick darkness. Worried that he would not be able to find the place again, he had the cabbie drive at a snail's pace. As he strained his eyes, the corner of the headlights caught the bright reflection of something that could belong to a motorcycle.

Shozo quickly had the driver stop and back up, then shine his lights on the spot.

"The victim's unconscious and needs to be moved. Sorry for the trouble, but I could use your help."

The cabbie, of late middle age and apparently accommodating disposition, cheerfully got out, though as they left the street and began tramping through the grass of the field, he shouted, "This area's supposed to be off-limits for night driving, but until recently there were dozens of bikers using it as a giant racetrack. And it didn't take anything to get 'em into a rumpus. They'd roar around playing music full blast. What were they thinking? They're not kids anymore—they ought to know better!"

He abruptly fell silent, as Shozo too stopped in his tracks. The motorcycle was still lying there, but the rider was sitting on the ground, having taken off her helmet and put it beside her, her arms folded over her raised knees and her chin resting in her hands. Looking up at the two men, she managed a smile.

"When did you regain consciousness?" Shozo called out.

"What—a girl!" the driver exclaimed.

She continued to smile. The face illuminated in the headlights was indeed hers, the face of the woman that Shozo had met in Harumi.

"Are you all right? You're not hurt?" he asked again, feeling mildly disappointed. While standing for half an hour at the side of the Bayshore Route in the hope of finding a taxi, he had imagined himself returning to the pitch-black field to rescue a critically injured or at least unconscious woman.

"I seem to have bashed my shoulder and twisted an ankle. My head hurts too. It feels heavy." She frowned as she spoke.

"These days even girls ride motorcycles, but such a big one? It's just crazy. A *man* could barely manage it!" The cabbie's tone suggested relief that the woman had sustained no serious injuries.

"You say your head aches. That's not good. You should get to a hospital immediately and have yourself examined."

Shozo went to her and offered his hand, which she docilely accepted, but when she stood up and tried to walk, she grimaced.

"My ankle . . ."

He took the helmet in one hand and ran the other under her arm and around to her back to hold her up. She was thinner and lighter than she had seemed.

"What would you have done if I hadn't come back with a taxi?"

"I would have sat here until the morning. Well, actually no. I knew you'd be back."

"How?"

She giggled and then exclaimed, "Ow, that hurts!" She was dragging her right leg.

The woman succeeded in getting into the taxi unassisted. Shozo gave the driver the address of a hospital. He had been treated there himself the previous year, when during a heavy snow storm he had slipped and fallen in front of his apartment building, which was located nearby. As they drove off, she whispered in his ear, "I was awake even before you went to get the taxi. I noticed you reaching for the zipper of my windbreaker, too."

"Then you weren't unconscious?" asked Shozo in amazement. What sort of woman was this?

"I came to right away. I wanted to see what you'd do."

He could feel her breath against his ear. For someone who had complained of a heavy and aching head, her voice was quite buoyant.

"Is it wise for you to be talking? You should close your eyes and be quiet."

The taxi was headed not for Shinagawa but rather in the opposite direction, toward Toyosu and then around to Harumi and Tsukishima. Factories, docks, and gas tanks cast an immense, unbroken chain of dismal shadows along the way. Leaning back in the seat, the woman obediently remained silent.

Shozo found himself in a strange mood. When he had been with the motionless black-clad woman out there in the dark field, her limp arms and legs outstretched, he had vividly felt the heaviness of her flesh, as though it were itself about to sink and decay into the reclaimed land. Now that she had regained consciousness, there was something about her words and behavior that struck him as unreal.

Perhaps it was that he had never spoken with a young woman in a private setting with such intimacy. More likely, however, it stemmed from the inkling that somehow her spirit had abruptly slipped out of her cadaverous body. Although she was clearly in her late twenties, she was talking like an adolescent girl. Moreover, her voice seemed unnaturally shrill. Yet, with the dirt clinging to the knees and elbows of her tightly fitting black clothing, this was, in fact, the woman who had been sprawled out on the grass.

"Aren't you going to ask me why I pretended to be unconscious?" Her mouth was again quite close to his ear.

"Because you're malicious."

"No, it's because I was interested in you. We've met before, haven't we? In Harumi. Do you remember?"

"I remember very well. It was the first time I came close to being run down by a woman on a motorcycle."

"And for me it was the first time to meet a man, more or less properly dressed, no longer young, and yet ambling about alone in the twilight on the Harumi Wharf. What, I often wondered afterwards, was he looking for, hanging around such a place. I had the feeling that he was probably looking for himself. You really gave that impression."

"You're one for making disagreeable remarks, aren't you!" But while those same words from the lips of anyone else might have been unpleasant, from hers they were amazingly not so.

"What a sight you were, sitting alone at the side of the road in the reclaimed land area!"

"You could see me even as you were driving at that speed?"

"Of course."

"In Harumi you said that you had to keep your eyes straight ahead to avoid accidents."

"Perhaps. But today I saw you. Really. I knew right away it was you. May I say something else?"

"Go ahead. I'm sure it won't be anything to make me happy."

"Something much worse," she said emphatically.

"How so?" He asked in all seriousness, despite his perfunctory air.

"You won't be able to get back."

"Get back where?" Shozo too had lowered his voice as he spoke.

"To your original self."

"Am I then a shadow-like being, a disembodied spirit, now willfully blundering about on my own?"

"Yes, perhaps."

She said this gently but with feeling—or that was how it seemed to him. Her words were surprisingly cool and yet at the same time sweeter than any he had ever heard.

The taxi passed through Tsukishima and came to Tsukiji. The streets were gradually becoming brighter with neon lights and street lamps. The woman had turned away from Shozo and was leaning back in the seat.

"Are you in pain?" he asked.

She shook her head ever so slightly, her eyes closed.

The Ginza was filled with light and crowds of people. Suddenly she looked drained of energy. As they arrived at the hospital, she made no further attempt to speak.

The receptionist told him that it was already past regular consultation hours. Nevertheless, Shozo pleaded that there had been an accident and persuaded her to summon the physician on night duty.

In a low voice that seemed to belong to someone else, the woman replied to the questions posed by the nurse in charge of making the patient chart. Shozo provided the physician with a simple general description of the accident, and then left the examination room.

As he sat alone in the dimly lit waiting room, he found it odd but not unnatural that he should be devoting himself with such zeal to a girl whose very name he didn't know. It had been a strange encounter, but he had the strong premonition that there had been a meaning to it, and though it quite escaped him, he now felt revitalized, as though the girl had passed on to him her own life force.

The physician came out and said that as the patient's brain-waves were slightly abnormal, he thought it advisable to have her stay overnight as an emergency case, so that a thorough examination could be conducted the next day. Shozo suggested that the woman's family should be notified, but the physician replied that she was apparently living alone.

When she emerged from the examination room, there was nothing left of the rollicking spirit she had displayed only a few minutes before. Her muddied, black riding outfit was as out of place in this hospital setting as a wetsuit would be on a diver wandering the streets of the city. Moreover, her face, which he could now see in the bright light, was heavily made up. Under the fluorescent illumination, it appeared quite pale and transparent, rendered all the more unnatural by the wild swirls around her eyes. It looked more like the makeup worn by kabuki actors.

"I'll come tomorrow to see how you're doing," said Shozo with a deliberately feigned air of cheerfulness, as he left the hospital.

7

The next morning Shozo left home earlier than usual in order to drop in at the hospital. When he asked to see the patient who had had the motorcycle accident the night before, the receptionist replied in a surly tone of voice, "What's your relationship to her? Are you a relative?"

"No. I happened to be there when the accident occurred and brought her here."

"So you don't know her?"

"No. As a matter of fact, I don't even know her name."

The receptionist consulted a card file and then said all the more coldly, "Yoko Hayashi is her name. She got up and left, without so much as a thank you."

"When?" asked Shozo, unconsciously speaking in a higher pitch. "During the night?"

"Probably early this morning. In the wee hours, we keep the doors locked."

"Why would she do that?"

"How should I know? Besides, that sort of behavior is common with these biker-gang types."

There was nothing more to be said. He too had the feeling that he had no reason to be surprised. Part of him wanted to laugh in amusement at it all, but he was nonetheless worried about the irregular brainwaves that the physician had mentioned the night before. At construction sites it was often said that serious symptoms would suddenly appear several days after an accident that had initially seemed innocuous.

He took the initial precaution of obtaining her address. It was in Shibaura.

"We can't vouch for that, you know. Or her name, for that matter."

Shozo paid the bill. It was no large amount. It occurred to him that he was embarked on a fool's errand, but he found nothing unpleasant in the thought. Rather, it put him in a euphoric frame of mind. The woman had disappeared as quickly as she had appeared; they were bound to meet again somewhere or other. The very fact that it had all been quite coincidental, or at least not of his own making, made it seem real and genuine. He was surprised that such notions came to him; he was, he thought, beginning to go mad, just as she had predicted.

At work Shozo attended several morning and afternoon meetings, where he frequently expressed himself with bright ideas. This was noted by his colleagues, attracting comments such as, "Well, *you're* certainly in good form today!"

Though his reply was no more than a faint chuckle, he was well aware of some inner stimulation. It was as though his spirit were acting quite on its own.

Once the meetings were over, he quickly took care of his remaining paperwork and left the company earlier than usual. The days were growing longer, and it was still light. The sidewalks were crowded with homeward-bound pedestrians. As they had now shed their overcoats, their apparel offered a fine display of varied colors.

Shozo passed the show window. In the daytime, the impression it left was not as intense as it had been that night, but it was still somehow distinct. In other displays mannequins were merely clothes stands, utilitarian objects more or less tastefully arranged. Only here were they arrayed in such a way as to appear human, strongly aware of both their own feelings and those of the other figures. Indeed, he had the sensation that they were baring the deep and dark stirrings of the heart—loneliness and reverie, suffering and longing—that lie beyond ordinary human consciousness. And yet it was only Shozo who paused before the window to gaze at the scene.

As he drew himself away, he felt the urge to go to Shibaura, even though the idea had not once occurred to him throughout the entire day. Was this why he had quickly finished up his work and left the office so early? His sense of being directed by an autonomous spirit within was both pleasant and eerie.

He raised his hand to signal a passing taxi. He was acting neither consciously nor entirely unconsciously. His state of mind was similar at dawn when, having just awoken, he sat in the desk chair of his study room; it was a feeling of dim, pale twilight, neither of night nor of day, neither of ongoing dreams nor of definite reality.

The driver turned around to him and told him that this was the general area of the address given. He could see only rows of huge warehouses. There wcre buildings that appeared to be warehouse companies, and a few people were on their way home from work, but the overall ambience was one of emptiness. He could not imagine a young woman living alone in such a place. Looking about, he could not see a single condominium or apartment building. Perhaps, just as the hospital receptionist had suggested, it was a false address, and yet it seemed unlikely that she would have chosen such a strange location as a fictional abode.

Shozo got out of the taxi. In the main road it was still light, but evening was already descending in the narrow alley between the warehouses. He asked a passerby for directions, mentioning the block number. "Somewhere in there," said the man, giving him a suspicious glance.

Shozo thanked him and walked on through an alley between two large buildings, until he came to the back. Here were rows of smaller warehouses, some of which were much older. He walked around for a while, checking his location on the address signs attached to the telephone poles. The sea appeared to be close by. He sensed the smell of the tide and the sound of ships' engines.

"It has to be here," he thought, but the building in front of which he stood was itself a warehouse—and an old one at that.

The iron front gate was securely locked. He stood there for a few moments, but there was no sign of anyone going in, coming out, or passing by.

To the side was a narrow staircase that led to the second floor. It was a simple construction of rusty iron sheeting and pipes. Shozo stoically went up. The rain had left reddish stains on the wall. When he reached the top, he found himself standing before a small iron door. Exposed to the sea wind, the paint had begun to peel.

He pushed and pulled the handle, but the door only rattled and would not open. The woman, he thought, had given a false address after all. Giving the handle one last strong shake, he turned to leave, but then the door quietly opened a few inches. There was no face to be seen, no sound to be heard.

Shozo turned back round and asked politely, "Is this the Hayashi residence?"

"No such person here!" he fully expected a deep male voice to growl. There was no immediate response, but then the door opened a fraction wider. And now there *was* a voice, that of a woman, low and husky, yet thin. It was not unlike hers but quite lacking its verve.

"Yes, Hayashi," the invisible woman said timidly.

"Yoko Hayashi?"

Again there was no answer, but the door remained open. The voice had been too young to be that of the mother. Shozo supposed her to be an elder sister but then thought that it would be highly unlikely for a family to be living in such a place.

At last she spoke. "Who are you?"

"I happened to be at the site of her recent accident. My name is Shozo Sakai. I took her to the hospital, but then she disappeared. If she's returned home, then I'll be happy to take my leave."

The door opened a little further. The figure of a woman suddenly stood out in the shadows. She was wearing a denim jacket and slacks. Her hair was casually tied back, and her completely unadorned face wore a tense expression. Shozo had the impression that he had seen her somewhere before, but the light that came in from the outside was too weak for him to distinguish her features with ease, and though a lamp appeared to be burning from far in the rear, she stood in semi-darkness.

"Come in," she said. Her voice was monotonous but not dull, dry but not cold. It filled him with a strange emotion, reverberating deep within him.

He went in, and the woman closed the door. The interior was dark and spaciously empty. In the back there was what appeared to be a prefab storage shed, in which a light was burning. Various things were piled up and strewn along the bare cement floor that ran from the entrance.

The woman walked slowly toward the back. Shozo's eyes quickly adjusted to the darkness. He was, it seemed to him, in the middle tier of the warehouse. On one side was a wall that reached as far as the ceiling, while on the other there was a broad opening down to the ground floor, as though he were standing on a ledge within a dark and bottomless cave.

He could vaguely make out a pile of white objects, some long and thin, others round. They were the dismembered parts of

mannequins: dozens of arms, torsos with and without heads, twisted legs.

Shozo suddenly realized: this woman, who had seemed so familiar to him, was the designer of the show windows.

As they entered the shed and he looked at her face once more, he was certain: the sharply defined features on her expressionless face, her hair pulled back to form a taut line at the edge of her forehead, the nervous look in her eyes, and the overall impression that hidden beneath this cold, hard surface was her inner being, writhing and churning, dark and dense. There was, however, also something wavering and nebulous about her, like a blurred or double-exposed photograph, though what this was he could not say.

"Who are you?" he started to ask, when with a frown she interrupted him.

"You mustn't meet that Yoko woman again."

What did she mean? He gasped for an instant before breathing slowly again.

The shed was in a state of disorder. The old table at which they sat facing each other had, like the chairs, lost its color. Marred with nicks and scratches, it was covered with plates, glasses, and sheets of paper on which designs had been scrawled. Other paper scraps and wire ends lay on the floor. Everywhere were drops of lacquer and paint, and in the air hung the faint odor of rot.

"You see, she's bad." In her voice was fear rather than hate. The lids of her downcast eyes twitched.

Shozo's reply was deliberately measured. "I find that difficult to believe."

"That's because men don't understand."

On the cheap wall panels hung crowded together a windbreaker, art reproductions, a calendar covered with red and blue marks, posters, various masks, birds and animals made of wire, and a plastic fish. From a corner of the floor rose bushlike plants of paper and plastic.

Shozo had the ominous and steadily growing feeling that here was a person who was more than a bit eccentric. No woman in her right mind would be living in the corner of a warehouse. What he found strange was less the chaotic clutter than her apparent need to draw everything at hand into her grasp and barricade herself inside it—like a bagworm constructing its case.

"What is your relationship to Yoko? Where is she?"

"She's not here," came the obstinate reply.

"Are you her sister?"

She was silent for several moments. Fleetingly glancing up at him, she turned away again and said, "In a way . . ."

Though the impressions he had of each were quite different, there was an overall resemblance between the two women in both body contour and facial features.

"Has she really not come home? She struck her head. There's a slight abnormality in her brainwaves that the doctor said needs to be properly examined. If she is your sister, then you should find her as soon as possible and have her looked at. I came here in the hope of telling her that. Doesn't she live with you?"

"No, and she isn't my sister."

"But you just said that she was."

"I only said that she is in a way my sister."

"What does that mean?"

"It has nothing to do with you."

Shozo had no idea what the woman was thinking. "If she isn't your sister, then you're hardly in any position to tell me that I may or may not see her."

"I'm telling you that for your own good."

"Why?"

"Because she's bad. And because it is men like you who are most at risk."

"As you can see, I'm hardly in my prime. At my age, I'm safe and clear when it comes to young women."

"Are you sure that's true?" she asked with what seemed to be a faint smile.

"And if not?"

"It would be your ruin."

"With the loss of family and fortune? Luckily, I have neither."

"I don't mean what you *have* but, quite literally, what you *are*."

"So a real witch of sorts . . ." Shozo started to laugh.

The woman sprang from her chair and, abruptly seizing a sheaf of papers with whose edges she had just been fiddling, slammed it down with full force upon the table. Where behind her hard, expressionless exterior had such violent emotion been hidden? Unthinking, Shozo half rose from his seat.

"I'm telling you! If you can't understand even that, then do as you please. Now go!"

Her tone was cold. Shozo stood up. For several moments they glared at each other.

"Do you remember me?" he asked softly.

"No."

"I saw you the other night, as you were decorating the show window."

"Really?"

"I like the display. I take a look at it every day when I go by. I don't know how to express myself, but I understand it. In any case, let's talk again. You said that I mustn't meet that woman Yoko but not that I shouldn't meet you."

She did not respond to his suggestion but timidly murmured, as he turned to go, "If you really understand it, so much the worse for you."

As he opened the door and went out onto the stairs, he saw between the huge, towering warehouses the reclaimed land, now slipping into darkness. Passing before him over the water was a passenger ship, with all of its portholes illuminated. Beyond it lay the Museum of Maritime Science, floating up as a white apparition from out of the gloom; still further into the distance would be Reclaimed Land Site #13.

He could not believe that twenty-four hours earlier he had been making his way hurriedly along a dark road in search of a taxi. Still more bizarre to him was the fact that he now stood on the staircase of this old warehouse. The thought even occurred to him that he was wandering in the dreams or delusions of another.

And if that were true, who was that other? The half-crazed young woman he had just left? In the depths of her cave she was constructing more hallucinatory sets, her mannequins as collaborators. Perhaps she was giving shape to their dreams.

Again he remembered the display she had made, with figures that inspired a sense of melancholy that was close to sorrow. Why did they continue to haunt him? Were they wondrous fantasies of matter that yearned to become human but could not? Or were they strange, semi-biological beings that kept only their outward appearance, even as they steadily ceased to be human? Such were Shozo's muddled musings.

He carefully descended the dark stairs, one step at a time, distinctly hearing each time the sound of his feet and feeling the solid metal beneath them. Yet his sense of treading empty space grew ever stronger. What did it all mean? he asked himself.

8

One week later, again on Sunday, Shozo found himself climbing the same rusted staircase.

The visit was not what he had in mind as he left his apartment; in fact, he had intended to visit the reclaimed land. He had not forgotten the warning of the "mannequin woman," as he privately referred to her, urging him not to meet the female motorcyclist, but whenever he recalled her almost threatening words, he found himself resisting them.

Knowing that the way there was more direct from Harumi via Toyosu than from Shinagawa, he went first to the Ginza for a light lunch. He disliked the ambience of the traffic-free pedestrian zones set aside on Sundays along the main thoroughfares. He was in search of an appealing restaurant in a side street, when what should he encounter but another of *her* designs.

It was built into the interior of a not very large travel bureau; the mannequins were arranged so as to be seen immediately through the windowpane. The display was of a smaller scale than that in the business district, but one glance was enough for the antennae of his unconscious—more than his eyes—to tell him that it was hers.

It was difficult to believe that the work of this deranged woman was in demand in such diverse places, but perhaps it was the mood of the times, at least in the strange megalopolis that is Tokyo. He remembered the assembly of young boys and girls he had seen some time before in Harumi. Had not they, too, been like mobile mannequins, walking silently about in their strange costumes?

No one else other than that woman could have created this strangely vivid, unique design, with mannequins more human than real humans, and plastic and vinyl forms more natural than the works of Nature.

The setting was a tropical island, with a man and a woman lying side by side in the grass. The plants were clearly made of vinyl materials, but the varied and bizarrely shaped leaves and stems, the spreading, winding vines, and the twisted stalks were all intertwined and overlapping in such a way as to suggest a viscous, dark green vitality. The half-naked mannequins lying in the shadows of the trees appeared to be bound together by innumerable tentacles of emotion, even though, in fact, no parts of their bodies were in contact. The wide-open pores in their raw, dry skin were hotly breathing.

The travel bureau was closed and there was no sign of anyone there, so Shozo pressed his forehead against the window and looked inside. His mind in turmoil, he gasped for breath. In the background, amid the tropical trees, a boy mannequin was playing a reed flute. His body had been painted dark brown, with only his eyes still white.

As he looked more carefully, he could see that the cosmetic cast of the female mannequin lying on her stomach bore an unmistakable resemblance to that of the motorcyclist: excessively heavy lipstick, that same kabuki stage makeup, and greenish eye shadow. She did not, however, have the rider's long hair; instead, she was bald, though this had the effect of making her seem all the more eerily carnal.

As the male mannequin had his back turned to him, Shozo could not see his face. With languid, half-closed eyes, the woman was smiling at the figure, but it seemed to Shozo that she was looking at *him*. He involuntarily drew back in alarm.

Though the light in the side street was already fading, it was still bright enough on this sunny afternoon. Yet to Shozo it seemed that all around him was growing dark and gradually closing in upon him. Sweat broke out on his forehead.

Written in bold letters and pasted diagonally on the glass door was the travel bureau's commercial slogan: "For all of you now wasting away in Concreteland, the Isle of Dreams is here!"

Shozo pulled himself away from the unseen power about to ensnare him and walked away. Even as the pedestrian paradises of the main thoroughfares were caught in the crush of crowds, quiet reigned in the side street, where along successive building walls only the bar signs were silently breathing. A filthy cat stuck its face from out of an alley.

Why am I so taken by everything that the mannequin woman makes? This eccentric woman, who barricades herself in an old warehouse . . . Is she not actually enticing me to meet the motorcyclist?

Shozo had the feeling that the mannequins in all the show windows, despite not having been made with him in mind, had each assumed her face and were laughing at him. He came out onto Namiki Avenue, caught a taxi, and told the driver, "To Shibaura."

He climbed the stairs to the top. Between the warehouses that lay before him was the sparkling, dazzling sea. Site #13 too was visible, and beyond it, rising thickly out of the haze, the Central Breakwater Reclaimed Land Site.

Shozo knocked on the iron door, but there was no answer. He continued to knock, now more forcefully. He did not wish to call out her name: attached to a genuine human being, it did not come easily to his lips. "Hello? Anyone home?" he called, and pushed lightly against the door. It squeaked open.

All was darkness. In a loud voice he again called out, "Hello? Anyone home?" He opened the door wider. Not even the light in the shed was burning. He took a step inside.

The light from outside shone on the concrete floor, covered with fine particles of dust and drops of oil. There was a faint, unidentifiable odor in the air of this vast and chilly emptiness. He shouted "No one here?" and a moment later heard the faint and trembling echo of his voice.

The thickness of the hard concrete, the intersecting iron reinforcement bars, a steel frame holding up the broad, high roof . . . Shozo had entered and walked around construction sites more times than he could count, but this was the first time he had felt so directly over the entire surface of his body the presence of cement and metal—their roughness and weight, their crushing oppression, the cracking sounds, the piercing smells, the colors of ash and rust, the bone-chilling cold.

They had demolished delicate, flimsy houses of wood and paper and destroyed moss-covered gardens, small and somber, to make way for an ongoing stream of office buildings, condominium and apartment complexes, factories, and elevated roads—all made with concrete and iron. They were certainly strong, stable, and even beautiful. *Yet have we done nothing more than throw cold and hard materials together and pile them up? Enclosed wall-to-wall interiors such as this, empty and frigid, quite like an abandoned mine . . . It is we who have first bestowed on our country this hermetically sealed darkness, desolate and dead, where even the strange-smelling air is stagnant.*

A loathsome feeling came over him. *I have built Tokyo from burned-out ruins to a great city. But I have thereby destroyed something invisible, including—as the woman biker so clearly told me—myself. Inside, the mannequins surely share in the void that reigns in this place.*

As though to block out the flood of thoughts and memories that were pouring in on him from the interior of this old warehouse, Shozo slowly edged backward and forcefully pulled open the door. The light from outside was dazzling; from the sea came moist and tepid air. He breathed deeply. His blood began to circulate slowly to every corner of his stiffened body.

His mind, however, was still feverish and agitated. If it was wrong to go on building concrete boxes, should one head for the countryside and cultivate the fields? Dig up bamboo shoots?

No, said an inner voice. *We have no choice but to continue coexisting with iron and concrete, plastic and vinyl.*

In a daze, he descended the staircase. That, it occurred to him, was precisely what the woman, buried away in her concrete cave, was thinking. She intended to bring the hollow mannequins to life, to breathe into them dreams. Was it because she herself was a mannequin? Her pale, nearly expressionless face, her incomprehensible utterances . . . *But am I not similar? Well now, it would certainly seem so!*

As he made his way down the stairs, Shozo moved his elbows mechanically, his knees jerking spasmodically.

Strangely enough, it seems to suit me.

He chuckled to himself.

On this Sunday afternoon there were no humans to be seen, only the concrete rows of warehouse walls. The sun falling between them painted on the asphalt clear-cut stripes of light and shadow. With a shudder, he felt the texture of the concrete pressing in. There was utter stillness. *Surely only mannequins are suited for walking here.*

Again imitating them, Shozo ambled on. The clatter of his steps echoed against the walls of the warehouses, his shadow hopping on the surface of the empty street.

9

The next Sunday, Shozo once more climbed the steps of the old warehouse.

On the door was a white plastic board to which self-adhesive letters had been neatly attached:

OFF-LIMITS TO HUMANS

In the lower left-hand corner had been drawn the picture of a small, naked mannequin.

Shozo spontaneously laughed. He remembered having done the same the week before and could not comprehend why this of all places should inspire mirth in him. Besides, he otherwise rarely laughed.

I shall go there, to the man-made island, to the soil that our garbage is forming. Is it not a new homeland for the likes of me, a man betwixt and between? That burial ground for the entropic waste excreted by Greater Tokyo . . . Yet perhaps the wilderness of weeds will in due course turn into an immense forest or an entirely new city, one that is more than mere stacks of concrete.

I shall seek that elven creature, that mysterious woman motorcyclist, in the vast counterfeit land that is her abode.

Shozo hurriedly left the warehouse area, caught a taxi, and headed straight toward the reclaimed land. The woman, however, had previously appeared only at near twilight, and though he had the driver take him into Site #13, there were no motorcyclists to be seen. In the short time since he had been there, the grass had all turned green. The area to the side of the road where she had lain was now verdant.

Had it really happened? He looked through the window at the passing fields, over which, haze-like, the rebounding sunlight shimmered faintly. His memory of the incident was less vivid than the panorama he had discovered the week before in a Ginza side street. The mannequin woman was more alive than his supposedly genuine recollection of the female motorcyclist. *If that night I had already seen what I saw then, I might simply have unzipped her windbreaker. Still, she said she was only pretending to have lost consciousness . . .*

As he thought about the figure of the smiling, bald mannequin, lying under the tropical trees, he felt his sense of reality being shaken to the core. "Isle of Dreams" . . . The island by that name in Koto Ward that had caused quite a stir more than ten years ago was now but a small corner of the reclaimed land. Whoever had come up with the name must have been wonderfully imaginative. Or perhaps bitingly cynical.

The taxi passed the Museum of Maritime Science where, with advancing spring, there were ever more sightseers with children in tow, then crossed the bridge over the Bayshore Route. The trees on both sides of the road had put forth hard, green, brine-beaten leaves. Shozo found himself unexpectedly moved by how even on artificial land, grass sprouted and trees grew. His response to natural hills and fields had almost always been devoid of deep emotion.

The ocean came into view, its calm and sunny surface contrasting with that of the choppy bay, where ships were constantly passing to and fro. Surfboards with small, primary-colored sails were riding the water.

"Is there a beach around here?" he asked the driver, who replied tersely, "Don't know. Don't come this way much."

Winding along those coastal waters, they came to a small artificial inlet, whose surrounding shores had been developed into something of a park. The South Sea ambience seemed to belie its location here in the middle of Tokyo Bay.

Shozo got out of the taxi. He had run up quite a fare, but his attitude toward money had changed. Especially since becoming a widower, he had, out of concern for his retirement years, unconsciously endeavored to spare expenses and boost his savings. Recently, however, his anxieties had markedly eased, and such went well beyond financial matters. He was in high spirits as he walked the banks of the inlet.

There were children fishing, but not in the numbers that he had seen thronging Harumi. There were a few young couples sitting on the grass above the shore, while on the ocean a dozen youths in bathing trunks were maneuvering their surf boards about; in their taciturn solitude, Shozo found something quite pleasing. For the less experienced among them, it could not be said that they were, in fact, "maneuvering" their boards, for these were readily overturned and their riders thrown into the water. Yet they seemed to take it all in stride, quickly righting their sails and setting out again. Shozo continued to gaze at them with unflagging fascination.

On the shore were only angular boulders, too large to wrap one's arms around. Shozo imagined that if sand were brought for a beach, this could be made quite a swimming area. The water was surprisingly transparent, perhaps because it was so shallow. The trees on the bank and the stones lapped by the waves were all too clearly from somewhere else, but with time they would acquire a fresh and distinct character of their own, a new sort of naturalness. He marveled that having until just recently been devoted to the beauty of the high-rises, his heart was now stirred by this modest cove.

When the last of the young people had returned to shore, Shozo stood up. The sun was beginning to set. The water had turned to a translucent gray, and the wind was still. The signs of nightfall descended, replete with a mood of desolation peculiar to the reclaimed land. *I am becoming addicted to this*, he thought. *Between nature and artifice, between day and night, between reality and fantasy* . . . From out of his inner depths emerged a hazy premonition of something about to happen. The invisible tentacles of his unconscious reached out into the dusk.

The mannequin woman in the old warehouse had warned him that any further encounter with the motorcyclist would spell his doom, but her words aroused no fear in him. Though at the time he had dismissed them as the prattle of a lunatic, he was now less certain. Indeed, he frequently had the same intuition himself. Quite without knowing how, he had somehow stumbled onto this land as though having been seduced. And now the decisive moment was at hand, the end result of the four decades he had lived since the time of the burned-out ruins.

This realization did not trouble him. Perhaps about to come into the light of day was that which, lying in the back of his mind, had sustained and driven him all during those decades. He had been timid, always seeking to weigh his options cautiously, but now that dark current within him had chosen the path that he must take and brought him to the place where he must be. And now this purely private, individual stream was seeking to merge with a larger one. Out of it came both the mannequin woman and the motorcyclist, not as mere phantoms but rather as living images.

Such were his vague thoughts as he slowly walked toward the Bayshore Route. There was no one left in sight. The trucks on the road were beginning to turn on their headlights. His mood was tense. *Why is it here on the reclaimed land that I become so attuned to my subliminal sensations?*

As he noticed a light coming swiftly toward him from a street adjacent to the expressway, Shozo thought it not the least unexpected. He had the feeling that his unconscious mind had summoned it or that he must somehow have known that this would happen. Nor was he surprised to see that the light came from a motorcycle and that astride it was the black-jacketed woman. She drew up alongside him and stopped quite matter-of-factly, as though by previous arrangement.

Contrary to his expectations, however, was the presence of another. Sitting behind her was a pint-sized lad in a baseball cap.

"A younger brother of sorts," she said.

The boy offered no greeting. Easily dwarfed by the two canvas bags tied around the rear seat of the machine, he was, to judge from his size, a fifth- or sixth-year primary-school pupil.

This was no place to ask her why she had absconded from the hospital. Such matters now belonged to distant, dreamlike memory. Shozo likewise said nothing of the warehouse in Shibaura. He sensed that the two of them on the motorcycle were bound by something quite distinct from any of that.

"You'll join us then?"

It was a question that clearly did not allow for *no* as an answer. Her voice was high.

"I'll come back for you when I've dropped off him and the luggage."

Leaving Shozo at the side of the road, the motorcycle sped off toward the cove, along the same road that had brought him here. Where might she be going? This was hardly the time of day for diversion along the shore. There in the twilight he stood in a state of tension, between anxiety and expectation, fear and excitement.

Her sprained ankle had apparently healed. And her head? She had looked so fragile in the light of the hospital room, but now she appeared to have bounced back to an uncanny state of health.

The motorcycle returned sooner than he had expected.

"Don't worry about a helmet. No one will see us. Up you get. Hang on tight to my waist, because I refuse to poke along."

It was quite as though she were issuing orders. No sooner was Shozo astride the machine than it bounded off. Reflexively, he found himself groping from behind for her waist, but he could not easily get a grip on the artificial leather of her apparel. When he tried to hold on lightly, his hands slipped, and he nearly tumbled off. Now he hastily clung to her, with fingers, palms, and wrists. Any sense of constraint about touching her with his chest instantly vanished. She was already bent forward, and he found his face awkwardly pressed against her lower back.

Judging by how quickly she had returned, the distance that they were to cover could not be great, but she nonetheless drove at what for Shozo was an incomprehensibly high speed. Though he shouted to her to slow down, it was clear that she could not hear him.

At least, he thought, no one could see him. His hands, which at first had instinctively gone to her hipbones, gradually came to grip her tightly around the abdomen. Her tense body was as firm as a man's.

He thought they must now be close to wherever she had left the boy, but far from slowing down, she was accelerating. Suddenly she turned left. With the centrifugal force pulling them to the right, he clung to her with all the strength that he had in the full length of his arms.

"Where are you going?" he compulsively shouted at her, though he knew that she could not hear him.

She turned toward Site #13. The broad road stretched out as a long, jet-black line into the obscurity. It felt many times wider, the asphalt now directly beneath him.

Entering the site, she again picked up speed. The air struck him in the face, so that he could not keep his eyes open. There was a moaning sound in his ears, the sleeves of his jacket and the cuffs of his trousers were fluttering so furiously that they seemed on verge of being torn, and he could feel the wind cutting straight through his clothing and into his skin. He pressed his face snugly against her backbone. Between the roar of the engine and the howling of the wind he could hear snatches of a birdlike shriek. It seemed to be that of a woman's laughter, but if no sound from her could penetrate the helmet, whose voice was it?

Her boundless self-confidence at the helm and the sheer massiveness of her machine made him forget any fear of a spill, but he could feel with his entire body that this direct exposure to the elements was entirely different from the experience of riding in an ordinary automobile. He was afraid. No matter how accustomed they might be to it, even those motorcycle rowdies must have the same sensation when traveling at such velocity.

Abruptly, she slowed down and came to a stop. As he raised his head, he could see soaring into the sky the jet-black ventilation tower of the seabed tunnel that led to the Central Breakwater Reclaimed Land Site. As though in an instant, they had flown to the end of the straight road passing through Site #13.

She tilted her motorcycle to put one foot down on the pavement, then, still seated, took off her helmet and burst out in unrestrained laughter. It was a shrill, husky laugh, like talons scratching the air. He staggered to the ground and walked around to stand catercorner to her.

"What's so funny? You go tearing along the road, with no concern for anyone else. That was my first time on a motorcycle."

Yet she did not seem to be laughing at Shozo's ungallant fear. She was rather releasing excess energy, energy pent up perhaps in Tokyo.

From out of the depths of the darkness appeared the Central Breakwater's fermenting mound of garbage and earth. *When garbage is gathered, it gives off heat. Cosmic dust gathers, forms stars, burns and shines . . .* Such irrelevant thoughts flitted through Shozo's mind. He intuitively sensed a mighty power, an uncanny law of nature, surpassing his understanding. It was even present in the mad laughter of this woman.

He asked her again, this time without shouting, as though addressing her for the first time, "What do you find so amusing?"

"I don't know. After barreling along like that, I always feel like laughing. Still, once I had you aboard, I was taking it easy."

The reclaimed land, it occurred to him, was an appropriate place for such absurd mirth.

In the headlight, the thick growth of weeds along the side of the road appeared startlingly fresh and green. And yet, rather than having sprung up on its own in natural soil, it seemed to be clinging desperately to the nutrient-poor ground. Her laughter too was not the natural expression of a young woman; it seemed instead to be closer to the cry of a dying bird.

"Was it fun?" Suddenly she had stopped laughing.

"To be honest, I was frightened, but I must say it was interesting."

"In the winter, it's even better. No matter how many layers of clothes you have on, you're frozen through. And then you notice that deep inside a teensy fire is burning." Her face was nearly invisible. Only the surface of her leather jacket was shining.

"How else do you spend your time?"

At this, her manner instantly shifted. "What does that have to do with you? If you're afraid, I'll leave you at the bus stop. The buses will still be running."

"No, I'd like to be with you. I won't ask any more questions."

"Really?"

"Really."

"All right then, that's better. You meander about and then find that somehow you've wandered out of Tokyo, but then, being on your own, you don't know where to go or what to do. You need me. And I like people like you, who have lived their lives and then strayed off the beaten track. I can't stand young men who talk tediously and persistently without having really lived. So will you come along?"

"Yes, I will."

He said this even though he remembered the mannequin woman's warning. *She openly says,* he told himself, *what I am already unconsciously thinking. It's not this strange girl I'm following but rather my own self, my real self.*

"Then get on. I'll take you somewhere interesting. You won't be able to change your mind along the way."

"Anywhere is fine with me."

In Tokyo that would never have been my reply. This strange land, its soil consisting of broken fish grills and single children's shoes, this ambience, both desolate and dense, where decay and generation merge, this darkness, replete with all its unidentifiable smells . . . That is what is inducing me to offer such an answer. This place where scrap and waste come to life again, where power flows in its circular course. A new world where, for all I know, mannequins come to life.

The woman drove even faster than before. This time Shozo wrapped both hands about her abdomen from the start, pressing his face against her back. Previously, he had only been a passenger; now he felt that he too was driving. *Were I to take a tumble, I would fall off clutching her. Why not?*

They were traveling not through the power of the engine but were rather being propelled by a greater force to which they were now joined, moving as an integral part of it. *That power is welling up from within me. And yet it is not mine. What a strange feeling! I am not moving in the least, but the ground is moving. The earth is rotating. The darkness that encircles the earth, the power that penetrates it . . .*

Before he knew it, they had left Site #13 behind them.

The sky above Tokyo was a murky red.

10

The motorcycle passed over the Bayshore Route and raced along the shore of the cove. It stopped where the pavement ended. In the darkness was the boy, together with the baggage.

The woman parked her machine at the edge of the road. Then she and the boy set off, their bundles dangling from their hands, Shozo helping with one. Neither she nor the boy spoke; Shozo too kept his silence, as he followed them along the faintly white path through the grass.

Soon they were led up an incline and, at the end of their climb, they found themselves atop an embankment surrounding an artificial island of sorts. Little could be seen in the gloom, but half appeared to be an open field, the rest a wood. They walked along the ridge, below whose outer side lay the sea. Beyond shone the lights of the city's center. Tokyo Tower, illuminated, was gleaming; the rows of high-rise windows burned yellow.

He was struck by the beauty, though now the sight did not, as before, spontaneously reach into the depths of his soul. Heavily pulsating through his body were instead the sensations impressed upon him by the darkness of the reclaimed land through which they had just passed. And that darkness was extending countless, invisible fibers into the vastness of the night.

He had nearly lost sight of the other two, when at last he found them again, now heading toward the dark wood, having climbed down where there was a gap in the embankment. Suddenly a light went on, flashing into the depths from tree to tree: it appeared that they had an electric torch. Although his eyes had become accustomed to the darkness, he was nonetheless obliged to watch his step.

The light stood still. The boy held it focused at the base of the trees, as she pushed aside some shrubbery.

"What are you doing?" he asked, but they remained with their backs to him, without replying.

"Here it is!" she called out, as she dragged out a bulky bundle from the bushes. "You take it," she said in an earnest tone, instead relieving Shozo of the canvas sack he had been carrying and walking on ahead of him.

If she can manage to walk through these trees with bags in both hands, he thought, *she's no doubt been here quite often.* The large bundle was not as heavy as it looked but was hard to lug, with two pole-like objects wrapped up in the thick fabric.

The boy walked behind Shozo, illuminating the way for him, but as they emerged from the wood, he turned off the flashlight. There was now an opening in the embankment, leading to the water's edge. A small wharf jutted out into the sea. They could hear the sound of the waves lapping against the shore.

The two stood at the foot of the wharf, as the boy nimbly began to untie the bundle that Shozo had been carrying. Seeing their state of tension, he posed no questions. In contrast to the artificial inlet at which he had gazed in the evening, the water's surface here was turbulent. When a ship passed between them and the opposite shore, astonishingly powerful waves beat against the wharf girders.

From out of the bundle appeared something soft and black. The boy took out a small cylindrical object from a bag; with experienced hands, undeterred by the darkness, he began to carry out his task. There was a swooshing sound of compressed air, and the black mass began to expand.

"It's all right? No leaks?" she asked in a soft voice.

The boy pushed the large, swollen mass into the water. It was a rubber boat. Once the two had thrown in the baggage, they half-crawled their way over the rocks to the edge of the water and got in.

"We're just like smugglers!" Shozo exclaimed with a laugh, only to be warned by the woman in a low voice: "Shush! Don't make a sound!"

The small rubber boat was filled to capacity with three people and their cargo. The two poles turned out to be paddles.

"Go!"

In the ocean, three or four hundred meters away, perhaps further, lay a small island. Shozo had had no idea that there was such a place.

"Why are we going in this way?"

"Because it's off-limits."

"Going there will mean we won't get back until the dead of night."

"We're not coming back."

"*What?*"

"Didn't you say that anywhere was fine with you?" She was quietly chuckling.

The boy had begun to paddle; Shozo joined him. Unlike a wooden boat with pointed prow, the rubber craft made slow progress. The water was a sticky gel, black and heavy. Soon his palms hurt; his shoulders were stiff. He wrapped his hands in a handkerchief and took off his jacket.

"Arm power isn't enough. You've got to throw your body into it and pull the paddle out with a real yank."

The boy had spoken for the first time. Shozo took him at his word and found that indeed he was taking less out of his arms. Moreover, the movement of his body was now in harmony with that of the boat, so that he had the feeling of gliding over the water rather than of slogging his way through it.

"When I look at you, I wonder just what you've been doing all your life," she cheerily remarked. "You haven't a clue about the essentials of survival."

Had it been thirty minutes? He didn't know with any certainty, as he couldn't see his watch. At last they were below the stone wall that surrounded the small island. Meanwhile the woman had taken over the boy's paddle. When Shozo let up on his, she said sternly, "We're going to the other side."

Shozo was exhausted, but she was still breathing normally. *What sort of person was she, this woman who, in the hospital, had spoken so softly, so timidly?*

"How about relieving him?" she asked the boy.

"I'm fine," Shozo bristled.

"Look, sweetie," she barked back. "Don't even think about putting on a show. You're ready to drop."

Her manner of speaking to him had shifted. He thought that the skin on his palms must be rubbing off, and he felt the burning sting of the saltwater. His spine seemed to be creaking, and now as the thought of how he would go to work in the morning passed through his mind, a sense of powerlessness suddenly vexed him. *What am I doing here?*

"If you want to turn back, you can always swim." As though having read his mind, she spoke in a tone of playful irony. "You could also swim to Tokyo. Over there, on the other side, lies Shibaura."

Shibaura. Perhaps the woman in the old warehouse there had been right after all. This woman burrows into the very crannies of my soul, gleefully wheedling and provoking me. But I cannot go back. The dauntingly high stone wall bore down on him.

Silently, he handed his paddle to the boy. As the boat moved along the wall, he sat hunched over, clenching his sore hands.

When they had first boarded the boat, the island had appeared no larger than a clump of earth, but now that they were alongside it, it was amazingly large. Over the long, high stone wall rose something black. Complete silence reigned, though the dense darkness was very much alive. Tokyo was now nearer to them, across the way; in spite of its lights, the sky over the city was dull and stagnant. Here the obscurity was even more intense than on the reclaimed land. It was as though this small island had drawn unto itself and swallowed up all the darkness that lay around, including that of the capital.

Will we likewise be sucked in and devoured? Shozo was seized by fear. Despite its stone enclosure, the island had the aura of a strange biological entity: a giant whale—no, an amorphous monster, a headless, tailless mass of black flesh, possessed only of a giant, all-consuming gullet.

The surface of the water was calmer and more viscous than when they had paddled in. Slowly but surely, the black rubber boat made its way forward.

11

"A real gullet!" thought Shozo.

They had reached their point of embarkation through a gap in an embankment, and now here too, on one corner of the island, lay a path through an enclosure. Yet nothing like a wharf could be seen; along the water's edge were only boulders and scattered chunks of cement. The stone-walled passageway was some three meters wide and ten meters long; beyond lay utter blackness.

The entrance faced directly toward the urban center, with Tokyo Tower and the lights of the Ginza immediately visible. Here they seemed to be right in the middle of that inner portion of Tokyo Bay through which cut the Bayshore Route. And in such a place was this uncanny, ghostlike island . . .

"No time for woolgathering!" the woman exclaimed as she unloaded the baggage onto the shore. "Secure the boat!"

Shozo tied it to a boulder with vinyl cords, the boy assisting him. They then walked into the entrance, carrying their belongings with them. To his surprise, there was so much debris about that he could scarcely find a place to step. Whenever he put a foot down, he heard the crack or squish of what appeared to be styrene and plastic containers, rubbish borne by the waves and swept into the interior of the passageway. Piles of what seemed to be instant food wrappings shone faintly white in the depths of the darkness. Again and again his shoes also crunched what felt like small, seashell-like objects.

They suddenly emerged from the passageway to find themselves standing at the edge of a forest. There was no path in sight, only dense clumps of tree trunks, with erratically extended branches and wildly overgrown leaves, embracing the boundless gloom.

The dull light of the Tokyo sky that had weakly guided their footsteps through the passageway was of no use here. The towering stone embankment that surrounded them prevented any movement of the air, if air it could be called: a stagnant pool of vapor, a blend of pungent plant odors, fragrant aromas, the smell of dripping resin, the gas of rotting leaves, and the humid fumes of the undergrowth.

"May I turn on the light?" the boy asked.

"Not yet," she replied.

The woman handed Shozo the bags and went ahead to clear the way through the thicket. The boy followed right behind her; then came Shozo, his upper body bent over, as he shielded his face with the two bags. The only sound he could hear was of the woman, as she parted leaves and broke twigs. On the ground lay decades-long layers of leaf mold, as soft to the tread as heaps of rice bran. The branches that the boy pushed aside would bend, then snap back sharply against Shozo.

"It's all right now," said the woman. The boy turned on the flashlight. The back of her jacket was illuminated, as were vines, twisting and dangling all about as though to reach out to grab her. Also floating into view were the huge, jagged leaves of tropical plants; along the edges, they had begun to wilt. The vines were creeping out along the ground from the roots of the trees.

"This is less a jungle than a primeval forest."

"So all the better, isn't it?"

"Whoever would have thought there could be a place like this, right under Tokyo's nose . . ."

With the flashlight they were able to find a way through the thick mass of tree trunks. And still they only needed to raise their heads ever so slightly to find their faces instantly caressed by dense, hanging leaves or showered by fine particles from dirt or dead insects. Suddenly looming into the light was the trunk of a tottering, withered tree, its rotten bark giving it the appearance of a mummy.

"Are we going in the right direction?" the woman asked, still looking straight ahead.

"We should be going a bit to the left."

Thoroughly disoriented, Shozo marveled at the lad's serenity. He was as unperturbed as though he were walking about his own house after a power outage.

"Aren't you afraid?" Shozo asked in a soft voice.

"Of what?" came the puzzled reply.

Ahead, around, and over them grew thick clusters of various leaves, branches, and vines. Slowly fluttering in the light of the torch was a huge, red moth.

"Look out for snakes," said the boy coolly, turning round to Shozo. "There are some poisonous ones that escaped from a ship carrying lauan from Borneo."

Shozo's nose was now accustomed to his surroundings, but his skin was becoming all the more acutely sensitive. It was not merely the enfolded and layered branches and vines that he felt, but also the respiration of their slow but ongoing, intertwining growth. In the soil, countless forms of small vermin and micro-organisms were wriggling and squirming. The pith of the rotting tree was constantly being eaten away by white worms, long and flabby. Somewhere would also be poisonous snakes. Copulating snails plopped down from above. The forest was stirring, the darkness breathing.

Under Shozo's feet was illuminated not a dead tree but rather what was clearly the work of human hands: the rotten remains of posts and boards, along with roof tiles.

"Be careful! That's the sort of place where you'll find snakes."

"What's *that*? The remains of a house, isn't it?"

"From a hundred years ago."

"A hundred years?" Shozo repeated in surprise.

"Didn't you know? This was a battery. Must be what's left from the fortifications that the shogunate threw together when Perry arrived in his black ships. Suppose this was a guard hut."

"You're certainly well informed."

"And there's too much you don't know," the woman interjected. "Children today know a hundred times as much as the likes of you, even if they don't read books."

"We're just about there," the boy said, as though he had seen something. Shozo could see only the overgrown trees, here in the midst of what was indeed a dense thicket. "If I were ordered to go back by myself," he thought, "I would never be able to find that passageway."

Still, he regretted nothing. He was even less inclined to abandon hope. The trees all around were exuding a vital energy, raw and intense, entering his pores and gradually permeating his entire body.

Something had surely melted, dissolved. It was a strange feeling, much like the one he had momentarily experienced flying along on the motorcycle over Site #13. It was the sensation of something seeping into him from outside, then mixing and blending with something surging out from his innermost being. He had the limpid intuition that these were one and the same thing. He felt intoxicated to the core, to a degree he had never known from any drinking bout. And yet it was not an unpleasant sense of nausea; it was rather a tingling sensation welling up within him. Together with the tree-dense darkness, the woman's hips were swaying in the light of the electric torch.

"Isn't this fun?!" the boy exclaimed in an animated voice. Hitherto mute-like in his taciturnity, he was now growing ever more energetic the deeper they moved into the interior of the island.

"They went to all the trouble to build the fortress, and then it was never used. In the end, nothing else will be left of Tokyo."

"What do you mean by that?"

Shozo had been listening quite seriously, but before the boy could reply, the woman called out, "We're here!" She sounded relieved indeed.

"I think I've cut my cheek on a sharp branch. It's bleeding. Look!"

The boy directed the light toward her face. Her hair, which somewhere along the way she had secured with a white band, was covered with dirt and debris. There were what appeared to be torn bits of cobweb stuck to her forehead, with tiny tree leaves entangled in them. The heavy makeup around her eyebrows and eyes, together with her lipstick, was gaudy, a thick coat of primary-color paint. And from one of her cheeks were flowing two or three rather substantial streams of blood, collecting on her chin and dripping onto the front of her jacket. In the dull, yellowish light, the blood looked almost black.

The boy rummaged about in the canvas bag that he had carried on his shoulder, took out something apparently medicinal, and went over to the woman.

"Bend down," he said. He tried at first to wipe away the blood with a handkerchief, but dabbing at the injured cheek only brought more, wetting his handkerchief black. Handing her the torch and putting his face next to hers, he sucked the blood from the wound, nimbly applied salve from the tube he had taken from his bag, and applied a sticking plaster. She remained crouched in front of him, directing the light at her face, her eyes steadily shut. Shozo had expected the boy to spit out the blood, but instead he appeared to have swallowed it.

Shozo looked on, feeling his heart palpitate without quite knowing why. The liquid oozing from her face appeared to be less like blood than viscous tree sap; it flowed down through the branches, trunks, vines, and roots, down through the boy and then back to the soil. Pressure from within his body was gradually increasing, as was heat from the back of his throat. She continued to crouch there, her eyes shut, lost in her own world.

Only the boy remained unruffled. Returning the salve to the bag, he took the flashlight from her and slowly pointed it about.

The forest came to an end; before them lay the embankment. Even here on this steep slope grew thickly intertwined plants, climbing and creeping, but contained within it was the clear form of a cave. The boy aimed the light in that direction. In fact, it was not a cave but rather a stone chamber, its walls consisting of the same heaped blocks of which the enclosure was made, the ceiling a rock slab, broad, thick, and flat. Cracks ran across the middle of the ceiling from the weight of the embankment above and the pressure of the tree roots, but it was easily high enough for an adult to stand, with slightly more substantial length. The floor was covered with dry grass.

"Just like last year!" the boy shouted.

"Well, yes, with no one coming here . . ." She was equally exhilarated.

The boy started to rush into the chamber but then stood still in front of the entrance.

"Seems it's here," he said in excitement. Placing his bag on the ground, he tiptoed toward the chamber, and with one hand gently shook a pile of dry grass. Emerging in the light of the torch, a dark gray, slithering snake appeared. As Shozo froze, the woman laughed, "Just an old friend of ours. Not poisonous."

The large serpent, well over a meter long, with beautiful, shining, mesh-pattern skin, crept slowly over the grass; unperturbed, it passed by where Shozo and the woman were standing. It did not even seem surprised when she bent down and stroked its back. Gliding leisurely on, it disappeared among the trees.

"It seems to have grown a size larger."

"It's shed its skin."

The boy reached into the grass, and, with his thumb and forefinger, pulled out the slough. Tinged with yellow and translucent, it had been quite neatly doffed.

"It kept watch for us."

He hung the skin, fastening one end to a crevice in the wall stones, then sat down on the grass, hugging his knees.

"Ah, it feels so good to be here!" he exclaimed.

Shozo recalled the mannequin woman's panorama in the business district, with the boy jumping out of the window into the night sky.

"Wish we could live here. We've got plenty of friends . . ."

Little by little, as he sat next to him on the grass, Shozo came to have the same feeling. The stone walls seemed solid enough, and he was no longer as sensitive to the pungent odors of the forest. Or rather it was that through his skin he was becoming aware of the intense aura slowly coursing through the trees and the surrounding darkness, quietly breathing as it went.

Although they were supposedly on an island, somewhere between the streets of Tokyo and the reclaimed land, he had the feeling of having descended into the depths, to the bottom of the whirlpool that those invisible, swirling forces had created between them. Even as all of Tokyo was producing waste and the reclaimed land was decomposing it, there was this blind, burgeoning power at work.

"By and by, Tokyo will become unlivable." The boy spoke as if he were talking about the weather.

"Why?"

"Don't know. It'll hollow out."

"Do you think it will be destroyed? Through war or earthquakes?"

"By something else, I think. There'll be a lot more high-rises, grand and beautiful, sparkling bright. But, mind you, there'll be no one there. There'll be nothing moving. It'll be, you know, like those souvenirs they sell, with sea bottoms or miniature landscapes, all enclosed in glass. Something like that."

"And when will this happen?"

"Don't know. It just appears to me in that way."

"Appears?"

The boy gave an affirmative grunt.

"He seems to be able to see and hear all sorts of things, but it's all nonsense, that sort of talk. What's more important now is that I'm hungry."

Having had the last word on the subject, she brought out canned and packaged food from her bag. They had a simple meal, eating from paper plates. When they were finished, the boy went outside and began waving at the sky.

The growth of trees in front of the stone chamber was sparser, making for a better view. Standing next to him, Shozo looked up but could see nothing.

"What are you doing? There's nothing there."

At that moment, several small, black shadows passed overhead like a gust of wind before whirling skyward.

"Bats. They know we're here."

Shozo could not quite catch sight of them, though he noticed the stars abruptly disappearing and reappearing. Whatever they were, flittering in and out among themselves, something was indeed throwing the heavens into confusion. The boy went on waving incessantly.

"There are all sorts of creatures here, aren't there?"

"Birds, mice, lizards, and plenty of bugs. The ones that can't fly here swim. Listen carefully! They're all moving about in the forest, because so many of them are animals of the night." He tilted his head slightly toward the trees. "There are even more invisible organisms. What we call 'soil' isn't dirt; it's something like a mass of fungi and bacteria. In a handful of soil there are a hundred million microbes."

"Can you see *them* too?"

"Only vaguely."

Shozo was hearing all of this for the first time. "I was already amazed at the stupendous growth of trees, but this . . ."

"Trees are only one part of it."

He sought to emulate the boy in his serenity, but despite his endeavors he immediately found himself in turmoil and confusion. And yet there were moments when suddenly he sensed how everything around him was filled with hidden stirring, breathing, quivering, slime-secreting . . . The darkness itself was alive.

"After all, there are tens of thousands of cells living in our bodies."

"Over ten billion!" the boy instantly replied.

The stirring came not only from without but also from within, and not from the soul but rather from flesh and fluids—from arms and legs, from belly and bowel. It was eerie, this feeling that the compartmentalized being he called himself was becoming soft and porous, dissolving into all that lay beyond. *I am passing away.*

And yet the sensation that his entire body was beginning to breathe in harmony with the pulsating movement outside himself also made him aware of a sweet pleasure he had never known before.

With the light now extinguished, the three sat talking on the grass in the stone chamber. Sometimes they were silent, though there was nothing in this that might have made them feel uneasy.

The boy burrowed himself into his sleeping bag, and soon there was the gentle sound of slumber. As though summoned, the woman and Shozo made their way into the forest. As they embraced in the shadow of a large tree, it was for him as though he were being conjoined not merely to a woman but rather to a vastly greater entity, and that their union was no partial intersection but rather perfect fusion.

They didn't speak; there was no need. The sap slowly flowing through trunks of the trees and through the veins of the leaves above also coursed through them, and the hot breath of the countless tiny creatures mingling and wriggling in the earth beneath them quite became their own.

In the rhythm of that unhurried flowing and mingling, their pulsating bodies were one with the fluctuating darkness: without consciousness, without labored breathing, without voice, without time.

Only once did it seem to Shozo that he heard directly next to them the sound of a snake, as it quietly slithered by.

12

Shozo was awakened by the sound of birds—a terrible sound, not of twittering or chirping but of shrieking. Not dozens but hundreds of birds, squawking hoarsely.

It was already morning, but in the stone chamber and in the depths of the forest, pale blue traces of the night remained. The boy lay peacefully in his sleeping bag; the woman slept, wrapped in a thin blanket and facing inward.

Closing his eyes again, Shozo lay in the grass, but the cry of the birds grew only more raucous. As though inured to it, the other two did not so much as roll over. Quietly, he got up and went out.

The forest that he was now seeing in the morning light for the first time was even more wildly and staggeringly luxuriant than he had imagined in the dark. He could not begin to guess how many species there were; these included tropical plants, resembling windmill palms, with broad, extended leaves. The furious struggle for survival, in which no human hand had intervened, had left an astonishing number bent and twisted, withering, dead and fallen, rotting.

Despite the protection of the surrounding embankment, the temperature of the morning air had fallen. Shozo turned up the collar of his jacket and climbed the sparsely wooded slope next to the stone chamber. The ground was rough, and he slipped and slid as he went, holding onto the creeping vines.

The cry of the birds was so loud that he could only assume they were thronging nearby, but in this he was wrong. From the top, he could see that although the trees were sparsest around the stone chamber, elsewhere on the embankment they were far denser—and that it was both from there, at some distance, and from the surrounding air that the sound came, as the birds circled in flight. Huge and white, they were apparently herons. A flock of them flew nearby, with flapping wings, their beaks and feet extended, nearly filling the sky.

Shozo could not fathom why they were shrieking, nor whether it was an extraordinary occurrence or a normal morning event. There was nonetheless something ill-omened about their clamor reverberating throughout the island. It was as if they—all of them—had been terrified into this state of agitation.

The sound was even more piercing than it had been inside the stone chamber, and as he watched them in their cycle, first perching on the branches of the trees, then rising up in great confusion, then descending once again, he felt their restlessness and anxiety being passed on to him as well. Any thought of moving closer was thwarted by the thick growth of trees and vines atop the embankment.

Just between the trees over which the herons were flying, he could catch a glimpse of the office buildings in downtown Tokyo. From out of the morning mist their upper stories rose like white gravestones.

"There's no way I can report my absence from work," Shozo mused, surprised at his own insouciance. It was not that he felt indifferent, but rather that the thought lacked any sort of reality.

When it had passed noon and he had still failed to appear, a junior employee would ever so gingerly make a call to his apartment. Shozo smiled, as he imagined the endless ringing of the telephone on the ornamental chest in his living room.

"He's never taken an unauthorized day off." "Could be he's suffered heart failure." "His wartime generation grew up undernourished, so their internal organs are defective. They aren't nearly as healthy as they look and then they drop dead without warning." All this talk on the part of his subordinates belonged to another world, to the distant shore, beyond the morning haze filled with the cries of herons.

He remembered the words of the boy, who had said he could see Tokyo eventually becoming hollow. Perhaps he meant not so much that human beings would disappear as that they would wind up transparent. Between the concrete buildings would pass to and fro only invisible electronic waves and bits of information . . .

He turned and saw that the water that they had secretly traversed in the night had begun to glisten. There was a further battery—similarly surrounded by a stone wall and embankment, but much larger than this one. Stretching out beyond it was the pale blue land of Site #13.

There I clung to her hips as we drove last night, marveled at the ghost ship as I first wandered about there alone, and went out to where they dispose of garbage. It seemed such a long time ago. *But ever since, that wild, artificial land has begun to possess me . . . And so it is that I find myself fallen into this place.* It was a dispassionate thought. *Might not be able to extricate myself after all . . .* Such was also his feeling.

Descending the embankment and again entering the stone chamber, he found the woman and the boy still asleep. He quietly lay down, remarking to himself that here cannon balls had been stored; as he closed his eyes, he smiled at the thought that he was now sleeping in what was left of an ammunition dump.

The cries of the herons were subsiding.

When Shozo awoke, the others were already up and about. The woman was cooking breakfast on an alcohol stove; the boy, bent over in a nearby cluster of trees, was poking about on the ground. The sun, already high in the sky, flashed through the leaves and branches, painting bright, mottled patterns on both the earth and the boy's back. The ominous shrieking had ceased; instead, all sorts of small, twittering birds were flitting about the forest.

Shozo lay for a while in the withered grass, listening to the chirping, gazing at the light filtering through the trees, and watching his companions from behind. Even though this should hardly have been a place conducive to a good night's rest, he couldn't remember having slept this well in years. He felt fresh and clear in both body and spirit. It had been a long time since anyone had breakfast waiting for him when he awoke, and that too gave him a heartwarming feeling.

"Ah, a good night's sleep!" he said to the woman, as he got up and brushed off the grass. "Even though I was awakened toward daybreak by the cawing of the birds . . ." His manner of speaking exuded a spontaneous feeling of affection.

"You're just in time. Let's eat."

Still bent over the stove, she called to the boy in a voice that startled Shozo. It was still husky and high-pitched, but its uncanny vitality had given way to a listlessness, as though of someone else. Shozo was reminded that he had never seen her in the daylight.

Standing next to her, he leaned over and spoke as though avoiding eye contact, "You don't seem well. Couldn't you sleep?"

"She's never at her best in the daytime," the boy said, an earnest expression on his face. "She's a night creature."

With his thumb and forefinger, Shozo removed the grass from her hair and back. She replied with a soft, single word of thanks.

As they ate, she continued to avoid any direct glances. He told himself that it was because she could not repair the thick and elaborate makeup of which she was so fond. Her lipstick was smeared; her eye-paint too was blurred and spread about. Her face was drained of color. In any case, there was no water for washing, and under such circumstances one could scarcely give heed to appearances. But the fact that she seemed to be bereft of all vitality caused him concern.

"Are you all right?"

"Yes," she replied, a half-attempted smile foiled by the tautness of her cheeks.

"The cries of the birds awakened me at daybreak," he said, turning to the boy. "I climbed to the top of the embankment and saw flocks of herons in the trees on the other side. They were all in commotion. What do you suppose it was?"

"Not just herons. There are seagulls too. But I haven't been there yet. Perhaps it was a snake going after their eggs that stirred them up." He paused, holding his plastic fork in the air, his face suggesting concentration. "There seems to be something wrong going on there. I have a bad feeling about it," he said with a frown. "I can't see clearly. Shall we go there?"

"We can't leave here anyway until it gets dark," said Shozo, then turned to her, "You don't seem to be doing so well. Stay here and take it easy."

"I'm going too," she replied obstinately. "I'm also concerned. And I don't want to be left alone."

Both her voice and her expression suggested some sort of inner struggle, an intense play of emotions. Again she seemed to him to be someone very different from the night before.

Having tidied up after their morning meal, the three set off. There was no longer any need to grope their way along. Through gaps in the overhead branches and leaves that in the darkness had seemed to enshroud them now shone the rays of the sun.

There was much bamboo grass. Past their feet scampered lizards. Startled worms dug themselves into the soil. The musty air was full of gas.

Shozo spontaneously took her hand. She held it with a steadily firmer grip, as though clinging to him. As she started to stumble over a creeping plant, he put his arms around her shoulders. But even that sensation was not the same as he had experienced in the darkness. Shozo began to ask himself whether everything might not have been a dream, that uncanny sense of dissolving into all the arboreal fluid and vital energy suffusing the island. The hand that he held had become damp with perspiration but was nonetheless oddly cold.

And now they came across a huge, withering tree, in its trunk a large hollow.

"The bats sleep here during the day," the boy whispered.

Soon they came to a clearing, where the sun was blazing. Covering this broad stretch of land were fallen, rotting trees—not the remains of living trees but rather man-made lumber: heaps of posts and boards, traces of their form still preserved, gradually turning to brown fragments. Here and there were scattered roof tiles, the remnants of a large house that obviously had not been torn down but rather had collapsed on its own and then been eroded by wind and weather.

The three of them wordlessly stared at the ruins; even in the bright light of the sun, they were dark, desolate, and as silent as the grave. The posts and boards, strewn in all directions, lay rotting atop one another. Mushrooms, brown and white, grew among them, with winged insects buzzing about. The otherwise tenacious vines had not, for whatever reason, extended their tendrils over the boards.

Shozo was filled with that sense of awe that comes with seeing something one ought not to see. Here was a place built by men, then gone to ruin, unbeknownst to the world. It was not like living trees succumbing to natural blight. He remembered the red girls' sports shoe he had seen at the garbage disposal site. If he had seen it deformed and decomposing ten meters beneath the earth, it would now be the same feeling.

This house must have been inhabited by samurai assigned to manning and maintaining the battery. Though Shozo had never been the least interested in such things, he thought he saw rising from the piles of scrap lumber the fears and anxieties of those men, haunted as they were by the sight of the black ships. Impossible as it was to imagine their nature and character, the story now oozing forth—of material crumbling to wood dust and becoming the food of mushrooms and insects—would itself die in a decade's time, when all had rotted away.

In the darkness he had thought that the island was full of vital energy, but here there was also a stealthy but steady dissolutive force. On reflection, he realized that this too was an artificial island, a small area of reclaimed land. Had there not been piles of styrene and plastic in the passageway near the inlet where they had left their boat?

Shozo surreptitiously peered at the woman beside him. In the night, fresh and vivid, filled with the power of a black wind blowing through the darkness, she was now like a mushroom exposed to the sun.

"Let's go," said Shozo, urging the others on. He was sure that they too had had an emotional response to the sight, but he had no idea what it might have been and dared not ask. The woman gripped his hand even more tightly than before; the boy was no longer peeking into the hollow of the withered tree.

Silently, the three set out again through the now darkened forest.

"Somehow I feel frightened," whispered the boy. "I'm seeing something strange."

Shozo could only see the branches and trees, through which the sunlight was flickering.

"Let's go," said the woman sharply and curtly. Despite the boy's apparent anxiety, she gave a strong tug to Shozo's hand and walked ahead, quickening her pace, as though something were summoning or drawing her onward.

The soil under their feet had changed from soft and moist humus to dry and coarse dirt. Thick trunks and dense foliage increasingly gave way to trees with small, sparse leaves on long and slender branches. They were now on the slope of the embankment.

Looking up, Shozo could see rows of high trees in which perched herons were folding and unfolding their wings. Some were slowly circling in the sky, but there were now incomparably fewer than in the morning and they were not cawing.

"The flock seems to have gone off in search of food, with the rest quietly staying behind. Apparently, it was nothing. I suppose I was wrong." There was a note of disappointment in his voice.

But the boy was visibly trembling. The woman had released Shozo's hand and was standing tense and motionless.

Grasping vines had relentlessly spread, twisting themselves round the thin-branched trees on the slope to form intricate net-like patterns.

Suddenly a tree next to them, one not much taller than they themselves, shook violently. Reflexively looking up, they saw a heron dangling head downward, struggling to free itself from the thin branches and vines in which it was entrapped.

"You've got yourself into a fine mess!" said Shozo, reaching out to part the entangled branches, as his companions looked on anxiously from behind him.

The boy took a knife from his pocket and handed it to him. He cut away some of the matted vines, even as the bird continued frantically to flap its wings. The trailing plants were thin but tenacious, and it was only after some effort that he had cleared away enough to allow the heron to pass through.

And still it dangled there, batting its wings without any hint of taking flight.

"Look! Around its feet!" The boy called out. "Strings! Lines!"

The long filament in which the heron's feet were caught was knotted and twisted in a complex web running through the branches of the trees all around. The bird was suspended upside down, its feet pointing upward, beyond Shozo's reach, and there was no taller tree that he might have climbed to get to them.

"It's no good," he said, taking a deep breath and lowering his arms. "We'd have to cut down the surrounding trees, and anyway, its feet and wings are broken."

The other two stared in silence, as the bird's power to carry on its useless struggle steadily subsided.

"Fishing line," the boy muttered. "It's thrown away, and then they get their feet tangled up in it along the shore or on the water. Nowadays it's made of strong nylon and hard to cut."

The boy looked around him, groaning as he went. Everywhere white, dot-like forms were hanging in the thicket.

As they climbed, they found still more; they needed to take only one or two steps into the shadow of the trees to renew their grim discovery. The slope was covered with dead herons, and seagulls too. And everywhere it was the same: their heads dangling downward, their feet caught in fishing line wrapped round the limbs of the trees.

"There and, oh, over there!" The boy sighed each time he parted the branches and found another.

A virtual scaffold. Small, white corpses suspended upside down.

The heron that they had first discovered had already stopped moving. All were contorted, their wings half-open, as though they had gone on flapping them until the very end; their long necks and feet hung in a strangely twisted shape, as if someone had wrung them.

None had decomposed to skeletal form, devoid of feathers and flesh, and though some had discolored touches of gray, their plumage was still white. Other than their black wingtips, so was the down of the seagulls.

These white birds . . . They moved Shozo to the core. Particularly the delicate herons struck him as life floating on air, as the embodiment of the soul.

And then these nylon lines. No creeping vines, no cotton or hemp fibers, but rather synthetic filament: a petrochemical product, thin, transparent, and resilient. In his mind's eye he saw the glistening outline of a petrochemical complex, bristling with towers and crisscrossed pipes, all sparkling silver. Behind it lay the shining pale high-rises of Tokyo.

"I had a foggy picture of various white shapes hanging down but had no idea they were birds," said the boy in a trembling voice. "I had only a choking, terrifying feeling . . . Let's cut the nylon and bury them."

"That would be difficult. There are so many. And we can't get to them." Shozo also felt that it was better to leave the dead birds as they were. *We must not hide them. At the very least, we three should not lose sight of them.* He seemed to hear these words spoken by a voice emanating from all around them.

The forest that had seemed to be the spirit of life itself was in reality an island of death. The place to which, by motorcycle and rubber boat, the woman had lured him was no teeming, wriggling, entangling, breathing isle of dreams, of birds and beasts, fish and insects. It was a new form of Nature, into whose depths oil, iron, concrete, styrene, and vinyl had already been absorbed.

Shozo pulled hard on the end of a nylon line that hung down from the body of an ensnarled seagull just above his reach. It swayed, quite like a dirty rag, squeezed and left to dry, and with it both the surrounding branches and, quite incredibly, the more distant branches. The line was terribly long. No matter how hard Shozo pulled, it merely dug into his fingers, without showing any sign of breaking.

Then from within the dense growth of thin, tangled boughs came a strange, bloodcurdling squawk. It was less a voice than a throttled gurgle: a piercing laugh, a convulsive sobbing, both human and birdlike.

Shozo and the boy hastily pushed their way through the branches. They found the woman standing in a darkened area of the thicket, where the boughs and vines were even more densely intertwined. Directly over her face swung a beautiful heron with half-open wings.

She was waving her arms, her palms pointing downward, her upper body swaying. In her tousled hair, the band still in place, clung bits of withered leaves; on her leather jacket glistened spider webs; and her boots were covered with dust. Shozo and the boy stared at her with bated breath.

In the trees at the top of the embankment, the clamor of the herons resumed. The sun, now at its zenith, was shining brighter than ever, but about the woman was a strong aura that seemed to be holding back the light. The movements of her body were ever more rapid and intense, even as her makeup began to stream down her face. Though seemingly not in a stupor, with glazed, upward-slanted eyes, she was obviously unaware of the others' presence.

In a muffled voice she went on squawking and cawing. For a moment, her features bore a contorted look of intense pain but then immediately took on a dreamlike expression, her eyes half-shut. Suddenly, with flashing eyes, she made a hissing sound between her teeth.

There in the heart of the thicket, less than a meter from the body of the heron, was a bowl-shaped nest, in which sat two beautiful, pale blue eggs, only slightly smaller than a mother hen's.

Shozo was trembling. "Does your sister often—?" he started to inquire in a hushed voice, only to be cut off.

"She's not my sister."

"No?"

"She's my sister but not my real sister."

"Have you a real sister, somewhere else?"

His ashen face stiffened. "No, she's here."

With that minimal response he went to the nest and picked up an egg, only in the same instant to replace it, as he uttered a cry.

"Cold! Horribly cold! Even the eggs are dead!"

The woman's voice fell silent; the convulsions of her body slackened. Her knees buckled; her arms fell. Slowly she sank to the ground.

13

The profusion of forsythia- and oleander-like bushes, with branches protruding directly out of the ground, left no room to lay her down. With Shozo taking her by the shoulders and the boy by the feet, they were somehow able to bear her as far as the base of a towering tree. Pulling and snatching at last year's dry grass and this year's fresh green weeds, they managed to form a bed to cushion her.

Her eyes were shut, her body limp and listless. Still, her breathing was more or less regular, as was her pulse. Shozo put his hand to her forehead; it felt warm but not feverish.

He and the boy sat down on either side of her, peering down into her face.

"Has this happened very often?" he asked in a low voice. "I mean, this sudden loss of consciousness."

The boy shook his head.

Her motorcycle spill on Site #13 had caused her to faint, but even in the darkness he had known that she was alive. Moreover, she had later admitted to having feigned unconsciousness. He had not been able to see her face under the helmet, but she had probably blacked out for only a few moments after the accident.

This, he thought, was different—and also somewhat different from what was usually understood as loss of consciousness. He even sensed that, far from being unaware, she was in a state of extreme excitement, of hyperconsciousness. Like a high-spinning top that appears to turn white, her mind had not clouded over but was rather incandescent.

All around the outer side of the embankment was the sea, and yet there was not a sound to be heard, neither of waves nor of ships. Sometimes there was the clamorous cry of the herons from atop the slope, but thereafter the silence was all the more intense. There was then only the faint humming of tiny insects flying about. Now just after noon, with the sunlight at its strongest, the entire area was enveloped in a thick, tepid blanket of plant odors, musty and sweet.

Shozo raised his eyes. The three of them were surrounded by the bodies of herons suspended upside down, here visible, there hidden. He could see nests, some empty, others containing eggs, whose pale blue was as strangely, eerily beautiful as the finest celadon.

Except in the dense shrubbery and here under the tree where they had laid her down, it was dazzlingly clear and bright. And yet the mood was tense, oppressive.

Shozo slapped her gently on the cheeks, but there was no reaction.

"I think she'll be fine. If she rests for a while . . . After all, it's not as though she banged her head or anything . . ." There was nothing else he could say.

Occasionally her eyelids twitched and her mouth moved. The two moved closer.

"It hurts! It hurts!" they heard her say. "Left dangling in the air . . ."

It appeared she was not talking about herself.

"The eggs are waiting." It was a hoarse, somber voice, that of an old woman.

Suddenly it was again her own high-pitched voice, "More, more! The top gear! Faster! More!"

Though her eyes were still closed, her skin was taut. There was the sound of grinding molars.

All color now gradually drained from her face. Her eyelids had stopped twitching, there were no more movements of her mouth, and her breathing became terribly faint. Her skin and the flesh beneath it contracted; her features changed. Her eyes slowly opened halfway and remained frozen, only the whites showing.

He seized her wrist in alarm. She still had a pulse, but her face was entirely expressionless, like a mask, a mask without eyeballs—no, like the face of a mannequin.

"Where have I seen this before?" he started to wonder, but at that moment it all vanished, and her breathing grew deeper. The look of pain returned, as the space between her eyebrows narrowed.

Though Shozo was endeavoring to control his emotions in the presence of the boy, his knees were beginning to shake. *Can a single human be possessed of so many interwoven, multi-lay-ered faces, voices, intimations, states of consciousness? Alternat-ing forces intrusively make their way into this woman's body and spirit—bloating, shrinking, twisting . . . From the beginning, there has been an uncertain aura about her, like a flickering shadow. Coming into the light, the contours of her body waver and fade away, as if those of another; in the darkness, she is preternaturally vibrant, brimming with life.*

That this was not the abnormality or weakness of this particu-lar woman's personality but rather, ruthlessly laid bare, the very nature of human existence, was a thought that startled Shozo.

I have forced myself to manifest only one form, one face, one voice, without ever really believing that such was either my entire being or my true self. Perhaps I have thus managed, by the skin of my teeth, to preserve some sort of identity—one that is, however, vulnerable to sudden transformation.

I had convinced myself that I had pursued my course not merely to be liked by others or to win their confidence—or so as not to lose my livelihood; that in the world of reality we are bound to our fate by invisible forces, and that to live is to accept it all. And yet this is not who I am; this face and this voice do not constitute my true self.

Shozo had unconsciously gripped the hand of the woman ly-ing there in the grass. Drained of blood and cold to the touch, it twitched sporadically and violently.

Until not long ago, I would have dismissed you as a lunatic, but now I am just like you. Such was Shozo's earnest thought. *Ever since I have begun wandering about on the reclaimed land, I have been shaken and pierced by various forces. My body is full of fis-sures, like those of a cracking mannequin.*

The boy was looking at Shozo's face. No, he was indeed looking toward him, but his gaze was fixed on something behind him. He gaped as though stupefied. Only his eyes shone, like those of a cat in the dark.

Shozo turned around.

The forest was absorbing the afternoon sunlight; the musty, stagnant air now quivered, holding all in its shimmering embrace. It was momentarily so clear that one could see the veins of each leaf, but then suddenly it was as though one were looking through a sheet of poor quality glass, the trunks and branches of the trees now strangely distorted. Other than that, there seemed to be nothing out of the ordinary. *It is the forest's humidity—or my eyes are simply tired.*

Shozo again turned toward the boy. "What do you see? Is there something there?" he asked with an edge in his voice. He felt short of breath, uneasy, as though the air pressure had abruptly changed. The boy did not reply. Perhaps he had not heard. He had opened his eyes even wider.

The woman moved. Her hand, still in Shozo's grip, shook spasmodically, and from her throat came a groan: "Dying. Everything is dying. Rotting."

Shozo hastily bent over her, but she sank again into slumber.

He quickly turned to the view behind him.

The entire forest was collapsing. The cause was neither an earthquake nor a whirlwind. In the sunlight that was shining as brightly as before, it silently fell, sinking to the ground like a tent whose supports have been removed. It was as though without warning all had been deprived of strength—the trunks to stand, the twigs to hold leaves, the leaves to spread, the vines to coil.

Shozo was speechless. He could only gulp and stare. In his hand, the fingers of the woman were clenched, desperately grasping.

The trees had neither fallen nor splintered; their brown bark was still like rough skin, their leaves still fresh and green, their branches still supple. Though they had lost their contours and were clinging in compact layers to the ground, they had not dissolved. No dust was rising; no torn-off leaves were flying about. The forest had entirely retained its essence and lost only its form. It had neither disintegrated nor decayed, but rather even more vividly asserted its all-enveloping presence—in the scent of fresh green, the sunlight-absorbing power, the dense stillness, the lithe force of life.

Even with the loss of form, one could recognize the slime of the white mushrooms. The worms were wriggling. One could distinguish the snakes according to how smoothly they slid along: beguiling, black-striped, liver brown or brilliant, mottled, darkish gray. And the lizards according to their speed: dashing, pausing, zigzagging off again.

Above it all blazed the dazzling sun.

The boy called out. His words were incomprehensible, perhaps even to himself. His entire body was trembling in wonder and astonishment, as though he were possessed. Shozo had the sensation, unmediated and palpable, of a desperate scream, an ardent expression of awe. Out of the depths of his heart, too, came the same voiceless cry.

Fear of disintegration, loathing of deformation. The forest was a forest and yet no forest at all. The trees, the grass, and the snakes had not been transformed into something else, and yet the trees did not possess the form of trees, nor the grass or the snakes their proper shape. The forest was nonetheless now all the more replete with a sylvan aura; a cauldron of life energy, it was terrifying, yet radiant, uncanny, yet beautiful.

In the boy's cry there was also something resembling a song.

Still vivid in Shozo's mind was the same sort of shock, incomprehensible even to himself, that he had experienced on just such a bright, clear afternoon, there, at the garbage disposal site. He remembered the light with which each of the various discarded items had shone and the power that produced an endless stream of waste, even as it created new ground—a landfill-generating power that would throw onto the scrap heap everything that Tokyo produced, and eventually even the city itself.

It was as in a dream, yet such a deep, fathomless dream that is experienced only rarely in life, when for an instant on awakening, one sees all of reality—including oneself—as a phantom.

As Shozo continued to struggle for breath, he felt that the cells in his body were shaking, quivering, scintillating.

Suddenly the woman groaned, writhing in pain. Returning to his senses, Shozo peered at her face. She took a few restless breaths, in and out, sharply grinding her teeth, then slowly opened her eyes.

"Are you awake?" He bent over and put his hands on her shoulders.

"Where are we? What are you doing?"

Shozo straightened up again. "You fainted. You saw the dead herons. So we brought you here."

She was still not fully conscious.

"And then suddenly it happened . . ." Shozo faltered as he spoke, and he turned around. A deep stillness had again fallen on the forest; once more, the sunlight filtering through the trees cast its mottled patterns.

"So what is it you say happened?" With an air of weariness, she sat up, running her fingers through her tousled hair.

"The forest disappeared," said the boy at last in a cramped voice.

"You two are both talking nonsense," she muttered, holding her head in her hands. "My head's splitting. Did I faint? I think I was having a terrible dream, but I can't remember any of it."

Shozo helped her to get up. She wobbled a little, but managed to stand. Frowning, she looked round at the dead herons and exclaimed: "Horrible! Horrible!"

The forest was as before, with its trees, vines, rotting branches, and lizards. But Shozo noted how differently he now perceived the thick trees and the dense foliage. Clearly remaining with him was a sense of having envisioned something, of having grasped that even this primeval forest would someday go to ruin—and that this might not be cause for sorrow.

14

Shozo took a week off from work, informing his company that he was having heart trouble. He started to explain that it was arrhythmia but was immediately told, "Don't leave anything to chance. See to it that you get well soon."

In saying that his condition was abnormal, he was not lying—yet the symptoms were quite the opposite of fatigue and depression. On returning from the fortress he had spent an entire day sleeping, but was promptly awake and alert the next morning. His appetite was good, too, and his spirits were buoyant.

Yet it was not exactly that he had regained vitality. It was more a feeling of having experienced violent diarrhea and being completely drained, so that the energy passing through him was not surging up from within but rather originated from outside, destroying something of himself as it went. That much was clear. Yet at the same time he felt that as this collided with his muscles, his bodily fluids, his fragmentary memories, it produced a faint light: the light of something bursting open, the heat of something beginning to decay.

Seated in the living room of his apartment, Shozo spent the day staring absentmindedly out on the street, lost in contemplation. There were few passersby in his neighborhood, an area that was clean and quiet with its many new condominium buildings. There was none of the usual bedding and laundry hung out on the balconies to air and piles of bric-a-brac. Here the glass doors were hung with lace curtains; the bright tiled walls reflected the sunlight.

He had long been fond of the streamlined shape of these buildings, the solid feeling of their reinforced concrete, their serene form and transparent stillness. Now, however, he knew that each building, indeed the entire street, was secreting, excreting, breathing. Every day it was discharging vast amounts of waste, even as it was moving toward becoming itself a huge pile of refuse. When he focused his view, he could sense that everything from the outer tiles to the inner steel rods was stealthily stirring.

Condominiums are built to last roughly sixty years. In fact, they might endure well beyond that time, but then there is the problem of how long, apart from the walls and the overall framework, the network of built-in water and gas lines would hold up. Not significantly longer than the human body. Thus exposed to atrophy, the concrete edifices breathe. Not only the rough walls of cement or mortar can breathe; so can even the surface of the hard tiles, for, like me, they are in fact filled with holes and cracks. They disgorge and devour all manner of things. In this, there is nothing unusual about concrete, nothing unusual about human beings.

In the evening, Shozo went out to eat in a nearby restaurant. The waiter, who knew him by sight, served him amiably with polite manners, a placid smile, and suitable conversation. Yet he had no idea what was really going through the young man's mind. If Shozo had asked him where he lived, what sort of girlfriend he had, how he spent his days off, he would have received a noncommittal response along with a smile. For his part, the waiter knew nothing of Shozo and likewise posed no questions.

They were both well-constructed show window mannequins, each playing here in the restaurant, half-consciously, half-unconsciously, his own particular role. *Banal it is indeed, yet very much a manifestation of this transient reality.* Clearly there is something that transcends it all, thought Shozo, as he remembered the forest within which the fortress lay.

Shozo took a taxi to Shibaura and mounted the steps of the old warehouse. *That woman will understand.*

He smiled as he saw the notice on the door: OFF-LIMITS TO HUMANS. He had the feeling of having returned from a distant journey. *I'm no longer human. I'm a mannequin who failed to become human, a bit of refuse now lurking about . . .*

She was there. After a single knock, the door opened. Inside, a naked electric bulb was burning. She appeared to be working. On the floor sprawled nude mannequins; in the dim light under the electric bulb, the smooth, flesh-colored bodies seemed strangely voluptuous.

"I seemed to have disturbed you."

"I was just about to take a break."

She had a low and nervous voice but with a hint of warmth. Her hair was tightly bound, her face showed no signs of makeup, and her clothes were of white, baggy cotton.

"I have been to a strange place."

"With that woman?"

"Something like your isle of dreams display. There's such a place not far away, right in the middle of Tokyo Bay."

"Oh? I don't know of it."

"You really don't?"

The two stood across from each other. A shadow of uneasiness flickered across her face but then instantly resumed its normal inscrutability.

"It is most certainly your isle of dreams."

"I don't know what you're talking about," she said in an irritated tone.

"It was delightful, truly delightful . . . But something else: is she really your sister?"

In his mind he pictured the woman before him with tousled hair and thick makeup. They were similar and yet somehow different.

Avoiding his gaze, she began to walk about the floor, her hands in the pockets of her pantaloon-like trousers.

"What were you making?"

"I'm in the process of killing a mannequin," she replied evenly.

"Where's the show window in which that scene will appear?"

"It's not a business project, just something for an exhibition I'm putting on with friends."

"But there's no reason to kill it, is there? It wants to live too—perhaps with greater sorrow and intensity than humans do."

"That's why I must kill it—for willfully going off on its own." Her voice was fraught with emotion.

"And that's not permitted?"

"It's horrible, loathsome! Like that woman!" She spoke in a powerful, hate-filled voice.

"Well then, simply hang it up by its feet."

"That's also an idea." She stopped and turned toward Shozo, a smile seeming to cross her face. "I think I had a dream of that sort. Something was hanging upside down. What might it have been? I can't remember."

"A heron," said Shozo, staring back at her.

"No, something much larger, like a human being. It was swaying there."

Her glazed eyes began to shine. From beneath her pale face appeared to come a bewitching power, the same magnetic force with which her show-window scenes were replete. Dreams in which, shut up in this concrete cave, she deliberately restrained, repressed, and condensed herself; visions that multiplied quite of their own accord. Into one so resolute on self-imprisonment, only evil forces could penetrate.

The woman suddenly moved briskly. Picking up a mannequin from the floor and holding it in both arms, she carried it to the wall, where she bound the ankles with a vinyl cord from a roll she had retrieved. Dragging over a stepladder, she used an electric drill to drive a thick screw into the cement wall. The vibrations traveled the floor to where Shozo was standing.

"I was only joking! You're surely not going to do it . . . !" he shouted at her, but she did not so much as turn around. The dark impulses fomenting in her had their physical effect on him as well.

She hooked the vinyl cord over the screw and began tugging on it. The mannequin slowly rose feet-first until, with its head above the floor, it was completely suspended against the wall. The weak light of the electric bulb fell short, so that form and shadow swayed in the dull, yellowish obscurity as the body of a naked human.

The end of the cord still in her hand, the woman burst out laughing, at first with a low, breathless rumble, then with a mad croaking sound.

Shozo quickly ran to her and tried to take the cord away from her. As she wriggled to free her hand from his grip, she let go, sending the mannequin plunging to the floor. The head was half lodged in the torso, one hand was broken, the legs were twisted, and a deep crack ran from the chest to the abdomen.

And still the woman went on laughing. Shozo slapped her on the cheek. He had never struck a woman before.

For an instant she opened her eyes wide and gasped but then laughed again. Out of her cackle, he could catch fragments of words.

"That is our true form. Twisted, cracked. Take a good look! That is you, too, however straight and proper you think you appear . . ."

Her laughter reverberated throughout the room, only to be absorbed by those same thick concrete walls.

"I think I also dreamed of lying in a forest at night, with you in my arms. But all I held was a mannequin here on the floor. Does the forest really exist? No, there are only two mannequins that collided with a thud and rolled onto the concrete."

Shozo left the warehouse without a word.

From the steps he gazed at the sea, but the reclaimed land and the fortress had sunk into the darkness and were invisible.

"The boy was right," he thought. "We should have buried the herons."

15

Every evening, as night was falling, Shozo waited by the artificial bay, not far from the battery, for the woman and the boy to appear on her motorcycle. Though a day, two days, and then three days went by without any sign of them, he was neither disappointed nor irritated. Once he would have thought it an intolerable waste of time, but now sitting alone on a bench in the coastal park and gazing at the failing light on the water and then beyond the road and the Bayshore Route to the desolate field of Site #13, already sinking into the darkness, he had the feeling of having slipped into a different stream of time.

Evidence of that temporal flow could be seen in the changing colors on the inlet's surface: from blue to violet, from violet to steel-gray. It did not seem to be a reflection of the sky's shifting hues; it was rather as though the water itself, in preparation for slumber, had undertaken its own transformation. Relaxing its rigid wariness of the sun and dissolving into the same obscurity was the reclaimed land, as if happily luxuriating in the low heat generated by the decomposing, fermenting waste deep within it. Shozo sensed that everything—the asphalt, the roadside weeds, the bench—had its own respiratory rhythm whether waking or dozing, and that these were subtly overlaying and reinforcing one another, creating a greater current of circular time.

Even as the rocks that formed the shore of the inlet were being constantly washed and eroded by the waves, the cells of the weeds were furiously dividing as never before. And in the soil brought from afar to create the reclaimed land, there were doubtlessly, as the boy had said, an incalculable number—billions and trillions—of microbes living out their short lives in a ceaselessly repeated cycle. Surely they did not lament the brevity of their allotted time. It was a strange and wondrous world, but Shozo was aware of how he was gradually opening his heart to accept its mystery.

Still, whenever he called up the horribly vivid, bloodcurdling memory of the swaying mannequin, suspended upside down against the dark warehouse wall, he felt a compelling need to bury the herons. *Unable as we are to release them to the sky, we can at least return them to the earth.*

On the fourth evening, as the night was beginning to enclose the reclaimed land in stillness, the powerful beam of a motorcycle headlight suddenly bore down on him from the direction of the Bayshore Route. The woman and the boy showed no sign of surprise at seeing him, and Shozo for his part said nothing of having waited for them.

Just as before, they dragged forth from its sequestered spot in the forest the bundle containing the rubber boat and made their way to the battery, taking turns at the paddles. They passed through the styrene-strewn opening in the embankment and emerged into the forest, which welcomed them with a gentle murmuring. Bats were zestfully flitting about.

It was only when they had sat down in the stone enclosure that Shozo announced, "Tomorrow let's bury the herons."

"But we weren't able to get at them."

"I've bought a small sickle that cuts quite well, along with a trowel."

The boy nodded but did not seem particularly pleased with the idea. "We'll have to be careful," he said, speaking as though he were already an adult. "The birds died in agony and so lay a curse on human beings."

"That's why we'll bury and pray for them."

When the boy was asleep, Shozo and the woman, again as before, made their way into the forest.

"I am very grateful to you," he said to her as they lay side by side in the dense grass. "You once told me that I was roaming about in search of something. I don't think I've found it, but I've come to feel and experience all sorts of things in a different way."

She did not reply.

"If I had not met you, I'm sure my life would have been wretched. Why, I'd have been nothing more than a mannequin in a neatly looped necktie."

Of the mannequin that had fallen from the wall and lain dead, twisted and broken, the other woman had screamed, "That is you, too . . ." But once again he thought that now it was all different. *I am a mannequin with breath coursing through my body—one who, even if lacking a soul, has permeating through him the power that engirdles the world.*

"Do you have an elder sister, who lives shut up in an old warehouse in Shibaura and putters about with mannequins?"

"No."

"I don't mean to pry into your background, and it has nothing to do with us here and now, but she seems to know a bit about you. She also resembles you in some way."

"I know nothing about it. I have no sister."

She spoke calmly and gave no impression of consciously lying. Yet the intuition remained that here was something beyond his grasp, something of which even the women concerned were not aware. *But it doesn't matter. It would seem that neither the workings of this world nor the human beings that inhabit it are what, until quite recently, I thought them to be.*

For a while he mutely gazed into the dark foliage above them. Unlike the other night, there was a slight wind. The overlapping leaves rustled, as though the murmur of the entire forest were stirring their hearts.

"About the herons," she abruptly began. "Wouldn't it be better to leave them as they are? There is something quite powerful at work there. I'm somehow worried."

"I feel so sorry for them, hanging as they are in the air like that."

"But you're now covered in cracks and fissures. All sorts of things have made their way into you. It's as though you were summoning them. You may *believe* that you are thinking and acting on your own, but . . . They say birds are at their most vulnerable when they are molting. You seem to be in a similar condition now."

Shozo thought that if it were anyone else speaking in this way, he would be angry. As though having read his mind, the woman continued, "I understand you well, for I too am one to wander over the reclaimed land in the twilight, quite like a shadow."

Squeezing her hand, Shozo laughed. "A shadow does not have such warm hands."

"You yourself must no longer believe that what you see and touch is real." The woman's voice was low, yet full of emotion.

He thought that she was right. *Even this forest suddenly collapses without making a sound, much like the herons that die, without knowing why, on thin, nearly invisible nylon lines. It is because the forest knows this that it is murmuring. And all that murmurs is now close to my heart. This forest, this small forgotten island, this landfill site born of rotting waste sinking into the earth, this hypersensitive boy, this woman . . .*

"I love you," he said, squeezing her hand once more. He then stood up.

The forest murmured all the more.

Night was giving way to the dawn, as the trees fell silent and the vitality of the woman visibly slumped. When Shozo once more declared his intention to go bury the herons, she did not strongly object.

This time she did not faint when the three reached the place of the dead herons. She seemed to be tautly focusing her mind.

The boy remained taciturn, but as Shozo cut a branch of appropriate length, attached the sickle to the end, and began cutting down the tangled vines, the nylon lines, and the thin branches, he unhesitatingly caught the bodies, straightened their bent necks and legs, smoothed their ruffled feathers, and closed their eyes.

In places the work was difficult. Shozo climbed a thick-trunked tree and from the side cut off branches with his out-stretched pole. The woman wrapped her arms around herself, as she stood there motionless.

"Sit down in the shade and take a rest," he called to her, but she only shook her head.

In search of more places where herons had died, Shozo and the boy steadily mounted the slope. Below they had already brought down seven, along with three seagulls, and by the time they reached the top, they had found four more bodies.

The sea stretched out below, sparkling in the bright sunlight; beyond lay rows of shining white office buildings. The ware-houses along the wharf in Shibaura were quite near; behind them soared Tokyo Tower and to the right the high-rises of the metropolitan nucleus, with the World Trade Center in the middle of it all.

"They really *are* beautiful!" was his immediate thought. Even those buildings whose walls at close range had a rough appear-ance were like highly polished silver plates when seen from afar, mirroring the clear sunlight.

"Magnificent!" he inadvertently exclaimed to the boy beside him. "Some of them were built by the company I work for. And we're building more."

The boy remained silent for a few moments, then let fall a single comment. "How do you suppose the dead birds might have seen them?"

Shozo was unable to reply. He lowered his eyes; soiled plumage from the dead birds clung to the backs of his hands. "How do *you* see them then?"

"As a gray concrete mountain covered with large dark blue stains."

"That is how you see them?"

"The edges are crumbling; yellow acid rain is endlessly falling," muttered the boy, as though in a daze.

This child, thought Shozo, *is seeing it all from the perspective of his present self. What I have just seen was through the eyes of my former self.*

He gazed again at the sight. The sunlight seemed to have dimmed ever so slightly, though the gleam of the high-rises, white and trim, was as brilliant as ever. *We built them in the midst of burned-out ruins*, he thought.

The memory of the refuse he had seen on the outer portion of the Central Breakwater flashed across his mind. *The rows of office buildings that have arisen by sucking and swallowing energy from the surrounding earth are becoming an immense cycling system, ceaselessly devouring dreams, disgorging waste, and bringing forth new land. If the forgotten fortress in the forest is a ghostly specter that at any moment may vanish, the white high-rises are rows of luminous shadows. When one day the vital energy of both ancient nature and today's city ebbs, there will be born on this artificial land, still desolate and half-formed, a new, sylvan city, a buoyantly breathing, inorganic forest, inhabited by mannequins come back to life.*

Shozo and the boy silently climbed down the slope.

The woman was watching over the row of birds on the ground.

Why is it, he found himself wondering, as he dug a line of fourteen small holes in the soil, that her sex seems better suited to looking after the dead? Into each recess, the boy laid the remains of a bird, while she put beside them the cold blue eggs that she had apparently gathered in the meantime.

As Shozo, trowel in hand, started to fill the holes, he was astonished to see that though the feathers of the birds as they lay in their graves ought to have been thoroughly stained and tarnished, they were still a pure and shining white. He saw a light more transparent than the sun entering the tiny craters in the soil and illuminating the pitiful forms, with their broken legs and wings. Over them lay the same radiance as he had seen over the discarded sports shoe. He could vividly imagine the birds leisurely flying the sky, suddenly descending to the water, or sitting motionless on their eggs.

As he contemplated how the power that produces an endless stream of waste and corpses, the power that breaks them down into minute substances, is likewise the power that brings forth new life, Shozo was burying various images of birds, one after another, in the ground. *Refuse illuminates the life of things, mannequins the dreams of humans . . .*

Standing apart from each other, the three remained for some time before the diminutive mounds, their heads bowed. In Shozo's mind, they were still constantly beating their wings. To his surprise, the vision gradually filled him less with a sad than a joyful feeling.

Finally, the woman said curtly, "Let's go."

"Is this all of them?"

"Let's go!" she repeated in a stronger tone.

"I think there are still some more on top of the embankment. It would be cruel to leave even one behind."

Shozo clambered up the slope. "I'll just take a look," he called back down. The woman was saying something inaudible, gesturing with her arms.

He looked down from the top of the embankment, but there was nothing white to be seen. He now looked up at a large, tall tree towering above him. On the small branches, he saw nests of matted twigs, and some five meters above the base was a thick bough, in the middle of which was the form of a suspended bird.

The bark of the tree was rough, with numerous stout vines winding up the trunk. It appeared easy to climb.

"There's only this one," he shouted down the slope. "I'll bring it right along."

Taking off his shoes and socks, he mounted the trunk. The tree was old and had various hollows here and there. Sticking his feet into these and gripping the vines, he made his way up. He had no sense of danger.

Straddling the bough, he inched his way along it. The bird hung nearly within his reach. Bending forward, he put out his hand.

At that moment, another bird came flying at him. With out-stretched wings, it gave a piercing screech. It was perhaps a mother bird, intent on protecting her nest from attack. She was not large enough to pose any direct danger to him, but when by reflex he straightened up, he lost his balance. Hastily reaching out his hands, he grabbed not the branch but instead a thick vine entwining it.

He was still holding on to it, when his upper body flipped over. As he tried instinctively to wrap his feet around the branch, other, loose vines entangled them, and the more his falling body pulled on the first one, the tighter they were bound. All of this took place in an instant; he had not even time to cry out.

The vine he was gripping gave way, so that he was now hanging upside down, completely perpendicular to the ground. He had no sense of fear, for he had no sense of reality, as though this were all occurring in a vacuum.

Blood suddenly collected beneath the base of his skull, and behind his eyelids was a furious, dark red swirl, which then burst and slowly dissipated into darkness.

Consciousness was fading. As though struggling to lift a steadily falling black curtain, he opened his eyes.

There on the opposite bank, directly in his line of vision, were the streets of Tokyo, the rows of high-rises all upside down.

Had his eyes grown dim? Or was the sun now under a cloud? The outline of the buildings faded into a single gray block.

Yet nothing seemed to have collapsed. On the contrary, be-tween the sky as eerily undulating sea and the earth as transpar-ent, empty sky, that gray block was wriggling and bulging forth from within.

It appeared as an immense mycelium, a mountain of gray mushrooms turned upside down.

The light is quickly fading. It is growing dark. The sky is an undulating black, the earth a transparent black. Only the topsy-turvy streets of Tokyo still shine—and ever brighter, in phosphorescent bright gray.

Floating faintly beyond them is the landscape of the burned-out ruins. Amid the pale brown expanse are collapsed walls, bare tree trunks, burning streetcars, a violently swirling sky, the sound of wailing voices . . .

It is no superimposed image. The ruins themselves have twisted, moved, and bulged, the silhouettes illuminated in the phosphorescent light, swelling and spreading of their own accord between the black sky and the empty earth.

Tears flow, falling over his forehead. Is it from sadness? Pain? Fear? The beauty of the phosphorescent light? He no longer knows.

Now all that remains is the rapturous sensation of being drawn into that ever growing block of gray.

16

After a month in hospital, Yoko Hayashi returned to her atelier in Shibaura. Her younger brother was sitting on the stairs, waiting for her.

"You're certainly well-informed, knowing I would be released today!" she exclaimed in an animated voice. It was a pleasant surprise.

The boy looked back at her as always with knitted brows, as though staring into the distance. "I just had the feeling . . ."

They walked side by side up the rusted staircase. The boy laughed on seeing the sign: OFF-LIMITS TO HUMANS.

"May *I* go in?"

"That's all finished and done with," she said, forcefully tearing off the notice and wadding it up in her hand.

The sunlight, now noticeably stronger, reflected off the rows of warehouses along the wharf with glaring brilliance. Shimmering between them in the distance was the reclaimed land. The light shining off the water too was dazzling. Of the battery, only a portion of the stone wall could be seen. The waves were quietly lapping the shore.

So placid was the scene that it seemed unbelievable what had actually occurred in that place. But, as Yoko reminded herself, it was nonetheless reality. *You must not run away. One of these days you must go there, though not for the moment, not until you have truly recovered yourself.*

Her heart began to pound as she put her hand to the door, but then, pinching her eyes shut, she resolutely pushed it open. She had left the door unlocked, as there was nothing there for a thief to take.

"Something smells," said the boy, as he followed her in. "Something rotten."

There was, in fact, nothing that might have gone bad in the course of a month. She had kept nothing fresh, resorting to either ready-made, store-bought food or restaurant fare. Her work materials were all artificial products, made of vinyl or plastic. And yet Yoko too detected something besides the smell of mold and mortar peculiar to the warehouse. *Perhaps it is the odor of what I have been up until now. It is as though I myself were lying among the mannequins sprawled there on the floor.*

"It's filthy!" said the boy without compunction.

"Workplaces are like that."

"I still don't like it."

"Let's rest for a while and then clean up."

She opened the door to let in light and air. The smell of the sea wafted its way through the room.

She went into the prefabricated room in the back, boiled water, and made instant coffee. Rummaging about, the boy found a can of cola and started to drink it.

"Does Mother know that you're here?"

The boy shook his head. "I'd like to live here too."

"There are no windows, and it's dark even during the daytime."

"That's fine with me. It'll be like being in a spaceship."

He said this in a cheery voice, as he looked about the empty, broad, dimly lit warehouse. "And you—you're quite well now?"

"Not quite."

Weeping and screaming under the body of Shozo Sakai as it hung from the branch of the tree atop the embankment, Yoko had returned to herself. To herself? Even now when the word came into her mind, she began to feel the stirrings of anxiety.

For some time before, she had sensed that she was possessed of a second self. She had lingering memories, fragmentary and dreamlike, of vague and disjointed scenes in which that person was riding about on a motorcycle. Later, when she underwent hypnosis in the hospital, she saw on video how, in voice, expression, and behavior she took on a different identity, and shuddered.

"You had gone much too far in shutting yourself off," said the doctor. "In the warehouse you associated only with your mannequins. What you repressed thus emerged as this other self."

Yet through repeated viewings of the video, she gradually became accustomed to the motorcyclist and was able to grasp that this behavior had, in fact, already been lurking deep within her dreams.

"You knew that I was ill, didn't you?" she asked the boy, who was beginning to clean up the untidy room.

"Mmm," the boy mumbled as a minimal response, then suddenly asked, "Won't we be able to go to the fortress anymore?"

"Well, *I* shall be going all right!"

"Oh come on! How could you possibly do it?" he laughed. "In a rubber boat over pitch-black water? It's not a park, you know!"

"But who do you think's already been there?"

"That wasn't you."

"Yes it was."

She said this emphatically, as though speaking to herself. *You must realize that that frivolous, foolhardy self, the one that slept with a man she hardly knew, was also you . . .*

It seems that Shozo Sakai shared those dreams that were deep within me, she thought. *I somehow knew that by unconscious intuition, and I tried to warn him.*

Yoko tried not to think about Shozo. Whenever she remembered him, she felt a sharp pang. *Is that love? I have never experienced such an emotion before.*

"You mustn't torment yourself with this," the doctor had succinctly said whenever the subject arose. "The link between your fantasies and the fate of this man is purely coincidental. Reality is reality; dreams are dreams."

Was that really true? Yoko still did not know. What, after all, is reality?

"The computer can go here and the video there," mumbled the boy, walking about the room. "The one for dubbing might go here, though getting it all connected may be a bit of a bother—"

"This is a warehouse!" Yoko said, turning to him. "Quite unhealthy."

"No, it's a spaceship, bringing ore from Alpha Centauri."

Human beings create reality through their dreams. Is there such a thing as a "true reality"? In the hospital, Yoko had actually given some thought to leaving this place when she was released and moving into a respectable apartment. Yet gradually the notion grew stronger in her that here might be where she was spinning out the dreams of her own reality.

"You must stop secluding yourself in the warehouse," the doctor had admonished her. "If you don't change your life, your alternate personality will continue to reemerge."

Perhaps. But it might also be true that reality no longer exists. There was something that had not come out of the mouth of the other Yoko, something that she had undoubtedly seen with her own eyes at the fortress. In the confusion of her memories, like the helter-skelter video images, that alone had remained clear and now came back to her.

She had seen the eyes of the dead Shozo Sakai. They had said he had died of acute cardioplegia brought on by shock. Even in death, as he hung upside down from the tree branch, his eyes were opened horribly wide.

"You know, in his eyes Tokyo was mirrored—upside down."

"You couldn't possibly have seen that."

Such was the boy's indifferent reply, but Yoko was nonetheless utterly convinced.

I shall climb the embankment once again and use a fisheye lens to photograph Tokyo turned upside down: the sea above, the sky beneath, and hanging in between the high-rises.

What that might reveal Yoko did not know, and yet deep in her mind thoughts were violently churning. It seemed that this image was of great importance to her. It was also as though Shozo Sakai, that strange and rare man, had in this way left the world a final message.

She thought back on the funeral, which she had furtively attended, accompanied by a nurse. Though held at a small temple, it was still quite a proper affair. One of Sakai's superiors, a man with a fine physique, delivered the eulogy in a clear and sonorous voice.

"You devoted your life to building a new Tokyo from burned-out ruins. And now we see here the most modern city in the world. Today, too, the high-rises that you loved tower majestically into the sky. They shine in the sun. True to your will and wish, we shall go on building more such buildings—even taller and more beautiful."

Standing behind the rows of mourners, Yoko had released a silent but incessant scream: "No! *No!*" Though she could not express the grounds for her protest, she could sense that in this her two personalities were one and the same.

"All right then. Let's live together, here in this warehouse."

It is here, this dreary, empty, gloomy place, where my new alternate self may well emerge: my Tokyo. Perhaps the day will come when I move into the city. And then again, perhaps not.

"No," said the boy, correcting her, "in this spaceship."

Here the child may foster his own dreams.

All that can be seen beyond the open door is white rebounding light.

KEIZO HINO (1929–2002) was born in Tokyo and accompanied his parents to Korea while the country was under Japanese control. After his return to Japan, he worked as a foreign correspondent for *Yomiuri Shimbun*, a Japanese newspaper. He later wrote several novels, his work being compared to that of J. G. Ballard.

CHARLES DE WOLF is a professor at Keio University. His translations include Ryunosuke Akutagawa's *Mandarins* for Archipelago Press.

PETROS ABATZOGLOU, *What Does Mrs. Freeman Want?*
MICHAL AJVAZ, *The Golden Age.*
The Other City.
PIERRE ALBERT-BIROT, *Grabinoulor.*
YUZ ALESHKOVSKY, *Kangaroo.*
FELIPE ALFAU, *Chromos.*
Locos.
IVAN ÂNGELO, *The Celebration.*
The Tower of Glass.
DAVID ANTIN, *Talking.*
ANTÓNIO LOBO ANTUNES, *Knowledge of Hell.*
ALAIN ARIAS-MISSON, *Theatre of Incest.*
IFTIKHAR ARIF AND WAQAS KHWAJA, EDS., *Modern Poetry of Pakistan.*
JOHN ASHBERY AND JAMES SCHUYLER, *A Nest of Ninnies.*
HEIMRAD BÄCKER, *transcript.*
DJUNA BARNES, *Ladies Almanack.*
Ryder.
JOHN BARTH, *LETTERS.*
Sabbatical.
DONALD BARTHELME, *The King.*
Paradise.
SVETISLAV BASARA, *Chinese Letter.*
RENÉ BELLETTO, *Dying.*
MARK BINELLI, *Sacco and Vanzetti Must Die!*
ANDREI BITOV, *Pushkin House.*
ANDREJ BLATNIK, *You Do Understand.*
LOUIS PAUL BOON, *Chapel Road.*
My Little War.
Summer in Termuren.
ROGER BOYLAN, *Killoyle.*
IGNÁCIO DE LOYOLA BRANDÃO, *Anonymous Celebrity.*
The Good-Bye Angel.
Teeth under the Sun.
Zero.
BONNIE BREMSER, *Troia: Mexican Memoirs.*
CHRISTINE BROOKE-ROSE, *Amalgamemnon.*
BRIGID BROPHY, *In Transit.*
MEREDITH BROSNAN, *Mr. Dynamite.*
GERALD L. BRUNS, *Modern Poetry and the Idea of Language.*
EVGENY BUNIMOVICH AND J. KATES, EDS., *Contemporary Russian Poetry: An Anthology.*
GABRIELLE BURTON, *Heartbreak Hotel.*
MICHEL BUTOR, *Degrees.*
Mobile.
Portrait of the Artist as a Young Ape.
G. CABRERA INFANTE, *Infante's Inferno.*
Three Trapped Tigers.
JULIETA CAMPOS, *The Fear of Losing Eurydice.*
ANNE CARSON, *Eros the Bittersweet.*
ORLY CASTEL-BLOOM, *Dolly City.*
CAMILO JOSÉ CELA, *Christ versus Arizona.*
The Family of Pascual Duarte.
The Hive.
LOUIS-FERDINAND CÉLINE, *Castle to Castle.*
Conversations with Professor Y.
London Bridge.

Normance.
North.
Rigadoon.
HUGO CHARTERIS, *The Tide Is Right.*
JEROME CHARYN, *The Tar Baby.*
MARC CHOLODENKO, *Mordechai Schamz.*
JOSHUA COHEN, *Witz.*
EMILY HOLMES COLEMAN, *The Shutter of Snow.*
ROBERT COOVER, *A Night at the Movies.*
STANLEY CRAWFORD, *Log of the S.S. The Mrs Unguentine.*
Some Instructions to My Wife.
ROBERT CREELEY, *Collected Prose.*
RENÉ CREVEL, *Putting My Foot in It.*
RALPH CUSACK, *Cadenza.*
SUSAN DAITCH, *L.C.*
Storytown.
NICHOLAS DELBANCO, *The Count of Concord.*
NIGEL DENNIS, *Cards of Identity.*
PETER DIMOCK, *A Short Rhetoric for Leaving the Family.*
ARIEL DORFMAN, *Konfidenz.*
COLEMAN DOWELL, *The Houses of Children.*
Island People.
Too Much Flesh and Jabez.
ARKADII DRAGOMOSHCHENKO, *Dust.*
RIKKI DUCORNET, *The Complete Butcher's Tales.*
The Fountains of Neptune.
The Jade Cabinet.
The One Marvelous Thing.
Phosphor in Dreamland.
The Stain.
The Word "Desire."
WILLIAM EASTLAKE, *The Bamboo Bed.*
Castle Keep.
Lyric of the Circle Heart.
JEAN ECHENOZ, *Chopin's Move.*
STANLEY ELKIN, *A Bad Man.*
Boswell: A Modern Comedy.
Criers and Kibitzers, Kibitzers and Criers.
The Dick Gibson Show.
The Franchiser.
George Mills.
The Living End.
The MacGuffin.
The Magic Kingdom.
Mrs. Ted Bliss.
The Rabbi of Lud.
Van Gogh's Room at Arles.
ANNIE ERNAUX, *Cleaned Out.*
LAUREN FAIRBANKS, *Muzzle Thyself.*
Sister Carrie.
LESLIE A. FIEDLER, *Love and Death in the American Novel.*
JUAN FILLOY, *Op Oloop.*
GUSTAVE FLAUBERT, *Bouvard and Pécuchet.*
KASS FLEISHER, *Talking out of School.*
FORD MADOX FORD, *The March of Literature.*
JON FOSSE, *Aliss at the Fire.*
Melancholy.

Max Frisch, *I'm Not Stiller.*
  Man in the Holocene.
Carlos Fuentes, *Christopher Unborn.*
  Distant Relations.
  Terra Nostra.
  Where the Air Is Clear.
Janice Galloway, *Foreign Parts.*
  The Trick Is to Keep Breathing.
William H. Gass, *Cartesian Sonata
  and Other Novellas.*
  Finding a Form.
  A Temple of Texts.
  The Tunnel.
  Willie Masters' Lonesome Wife.
Gérard Gavarry, *Hoppla! 1 2 3.*
Etienne Gilson,
  The Arts of the Beautiful.
  Forms and Substances in the Arts.
C. S. Giscombe, *Giscome Road.*
  Here.
  Prairie Style.
Douglas Glover, *Bad News of the Heart.*
  The Enamoured Knight.
Witold Gombrowicz,
  A Kind of Testament.
Karen Elizabeth Gordon,
  The Red Shoes.
Georgi Gospodinov, *Natural Novel.*
Juan Goytisolo, *Count Julian.*
  Juan the Landless.
  Makbara.
  Marks of Identity.
Patrick Grainville, *The Cave of Heaven.*
Henry Green, *Back.*
  Blindness.
  Concluding.
  Doting.
  Nothing.
Jiří Gruša, *The Questionnaire.*
Gabriel Gudding,
  Rhode Island Notebook.
Mela Hartwig, *Am I a Redundant
  Human Being?*
John Hawkes, *The Passion Artist.*
  Whistlejacket.
Aleksandar Hemon, ed.,
  Best European Fiction.
Aidan Higgins, *A Bestiary.*
  Balcony of Europe.
  Bornholm Night-Ferry.
  Darkling Plain: Texts for the Air.
  Flotsam and Jetsam.
  Langrishe, Go Down.
  Scenes from a Receding Past.
  Windy Arbours.
Keizo Hino, *Isle of Dreams.*
Aldous Huxley, *Antic Hay.*
  Crome Yellow.
  Point Counter Point.
  Those Barren Leaves.
  Time Must Have a Stop.
Mikhail Iossel and Jeff Parker, eds.,
  *Amerika: Russian Writers View the
  United States.*
Gert Jonke, *The Distant Sound.*
  Geometric Regional Novel.

Homage to Czerny.
  The System of Vienna.
Jacques Jouet, *Mountain R.*
  Savage.
Charles Juliet, *Conversations with
  Samuel Beckett and Bram van
  Velde.*
Mieko Kanai, *The Word Book.*
Yoram Kaniuk, *Life on Sandpaper.*
Hugh Kenner, *The Counterfeiters.*
  *Flaubert, Joyce and Beckett:
  The Stoic Comedians.*
  Joyce's Voices.
Danilo Kiš, *Garden, Ashes.*
  A Tomb for Boris Davidovich.
Anita Konkka, *A Fool's Paradise.*
George Konrád, *The City Builder.*
Tadeusz Konwicki, *A Minor Apocalypse.*
  The Polish Complex.
Menis Koumandareas, *Koula.*
Elaine Kraf, *The Princess of 72nd Street.*
Jim Krusoe, *Iceland.*
Ewa Kuryluk, *Century 21.*
Emilio Lascano Tegui, *On Elegance
  While Sleeping.*
Eric Laurrent, *Do Not Touch.*
Violette Leduc, *La Bâtarde.*
Suzanne Jill Levine, *The Subversive
  Scribe: Translating Latin
  American Fiction.*
Deborah Levy, *Billy and Girl.*
  *Pillow Talk in Europe and Other
  Places.*
José Lezama Lima, *Paradiso.*
Rosa Liksom, *Dark Paradise.*
Osman Lins, *Avalovara.*
  The Queen of the Prisons of Greece.
Alf Mac Lochlainn,
  The Corpus in the Library.
  Out of Focus.
Ron Loewinsohn, *Magnetic Field(s).*
Brian Lynch, *The Winner of Sorrow.*
D. Keith Mano, *Take Five.*
Micheline Aharonian Marcom,
  The Mirror in the Well.
Ben Marcus,
  The Age of Wire and String.
Wallace Markfield,
  Teitlebaum's Window.
  To an Early Grave.
David Markson, *Reader's Block.*
  Springer's Progress.
  Wittgenstein's Mistress.
Carole Maso, *AVA.*
Ladislav Matejka and Krystyna
  Pomorska, eds.,
  *Readings in Russian Poetics:
  Formalist and Structuralist Views.*
Harry Mathews,
  *The Case of the Persevering Maltese:
  Collected Essays.*
  Cigarettes.
  The Conversions.
  *The Human Country: New and
  Collected Stories.*
  The Journalist.

My Life in CIA.
Singular Pleasures.
The Sinking of the Odradek
   Stadium.
Tlooth.
20 Lines a Day.
JOSEPH McELROY,
   Night Soul and Other Stories.
ROBERT L. McLAUGHLIN, ED.,
   Innovations: An Anthology of
   Modern & Contemporary Fiction.
HERMAN MELVILLE, *The Confidence-Man.*
AMANDA MICHALOPOULOU, *I'd Like.*
STEVEN MILLHAUSER,
   The Barnum Museum.
   In the Penny Arcade.
RALPH J. MILLS, JR.,
   Essays on Poetry.
MOMUS, *The Book of Jokes.*
CHRISTINE MONTALBETTI, *Western.*
OLIVE MOORE, *Spleen.*
NICHOLAS MOSLEY, *Accident.*
   Assassins.
   Catastrophe Practice.
   Children of Darkness and Light.
   Experience and Religion.
   God's Hazard.
   The Hesperides Tree.
   Hopeful Monsters.
   Imago Bird.
   Impossible Object.
   Inventing God.
   Judith.
   Look at the Dark.
   Natalie Natalia.
   Paradoxes of Peace.
   Serpent.
   Time at War.
   The Uses of Slime Mould:
   Essays of Four Decades.
WARREN MOTTE,
   Fables of the Novel: French Fiction
   since 1990.
   Fiction Now: The French Novel in
   the 21st Century.
   Oulipo: A Primer of Potential
   Literature.
YVES NAVARRE, *Our Share of Time.*
   Sweet Tooth.
DOROTHY NELSON, *In Night's City.*
   Tar and Feathers.
ESHKOL NEVO, *Homesick.*
WILFRIDO D. NOLLEDO,
   But for the Lovers.
FLANN O'BRIEN,
   At Swim-Two-Birds.
   At War.
   The Best of Myles.
   The Dalkey Archive.
   Further Cuttings.
   The Hard Life.
   The Poor Mouth.
   The Third Policeman.
CLAUDE OLLIER, *The Mise-en-Scène.*
PATRIK OUŘEDNÍK, *Europeana.*
BORIS PAHOR, *Necropolis.*

FERNANDO DEL PASO,
   News from the Empire.
   Palinuro of Mexico.
ROBERT PINGET, *The Inquisitory.*
   Mahu or The Material.
   Trio.
MANUEL PUIG,
   Betrayed by Rita Hayworth.
   The Buenos Aires Affair.
   Heartbreak Tango.
RAYMOND QUENEAU, *The Last Days.*
   Odile.
   Pierrot Mon Ami.
   Saint Glinglin.
ANN QUIN, *Berg.*
   Passages.
   Three.
   Tripticks.
ISHMAEL REED,
   The Free-Lance Pallbearers.
   The Last Days of Louisiana Red.
   Ishmael Reed: The Plays.
   Reckless Eyeballing.
   The Terrible Threes.
   The Terrible Twos.
   Yellow Back Radio Broke-Down.
JEAN RICARDOU, *Place Names.*
RAINER MARIA RILKE, *The Notebooks of*
   Malte Laurids Brigge.
JULIÁN RÍOS, *The House of Ulysses.*
   Larva: A Midsummer Night's Babel.
   Poundemonium.
AUGUSTO ROA BASTOS, *I the Supreme.*
DANIËL ROBBERECHTS,
   Arriving in Avignon.
OLIVIER ROLIN, *Hotel Crystal.*
ALIX CLEO ROUBAUD, *Alix's Journal.*
JACQUES ROUBAUD, *The Form of a*
   City Changes Faster, Alas, Than
   the Human Heart.
   The Great Fire of London.
   Hortense in Exile.
   Hortense Is Abducted.
   The Loop.
   The Plurality of Worlds of Lewis.
   The Princess Hoppy.
   Some Thing Black.
LEON S. ROUDIEZ,
   French Fiction Revisited.
VEDRANA RUDAN, *Night.*
STIG SÆTERBAKKEN, *Siamese.*
LYDIE SALVAYRE, *The Company of Ghosts.*
   Everyday Life.
   The Lecture.
   Portrait of the Writer as a
   Domesticated Animal.
   The Power of Flies.
LUIS RAFAEL SÁNCHEZ,
   Macho Camacho's Beat.
SEVERO SARDUY, *Cobra & Maitreya.*
NATHALIE SARRAUTE,
   Do You Hear Them?
   Martereau.
   The Planetarium.
ARNO SCHMIDT, *Collected Stories.*
   Nobodaddy's Children.

CHRISTINE SCHUTT, *Nightwork.*
GAIL SCOTT, *My Paris.*
DAMION SEARLS, *What We Were Doing and Where We Were Going.*
JUNE AKERS SEESE,
Is This What Other Women Feel Too?
What Waiting Really Means.
BERNARD SHARE, *Inish.*
Transit.
AURELIE SHEEHAN,
Jack Kerouac Is Pregnant.
VIKTOR SHKLOVSKY, *Knight's Move.*
A Sentimental Journey:
Memoirs 1917–1922.
Energy of Delusion: A Book on Plot.
Literature and Cinematography.
Theory of Prose.
Third Factory.
Zoo, or Letters Not about Love.
CLAUDE SIMON, *The Invitation.*
PIERRE SINIAC, *The Collaborators.*
JOSEF ŠKVORECKÝ, *The Engineer of Human Souls.*
GILBERT SORRENTINO,
Aberration of Starlight.
Blue Pastoral.
Crystal Vision.
Imaginative Qualities of Actual Things.
Mulligan Stew.
Pack of Lies.
Red the Fiend.
The Sky Changes.
Something Said.
Splendide-Hôtel.
Steelwork.
Under the Shadow.
W. M. SPACKMAN,
The Complete Fiction.
ANDRZEJ STASIUK, *Fado.*
GERTRUDE STEIN,
Lucy Church Amiably.
The Making of Americans.
A Novel of Thank You.
LARS SVENDSEN, *A Philosophy of Evil.*
PIOTR SZEWC, *Annihilation.*
GONÇALO M. TAVARES, *Jerusalem.*
LUCIAN DAN TEODOROVICI,
Our Circus Presents . . .
STEFAN THEMERSON, *Hobson's Island.*
The Mystery of the Sardine.
Tom Harris.
JOHN TOOMEY, *Sleepwalker.*
JEAN-PHILIPPE TOUSSAINT,
The Bathroom.
Camera.
Monsieur.
Running Away.
Self-Portrait Abroad.
Television.
DUMITRU TSEPENEAG,
Hotel Europa.
The Necessary Marriage.
Pigeon Post.
Vain Art of the Fugue.
ESTHER TUSQUETS, *Stranded.*

DUBRAVKA UGRESIC,
Lend Me Your Character.
Thank You for Not Reading.
MATI UNT, *Brecht at Night.*
Diary of a Blood Donor.
Things in the Night.
ÁLVARO URIBE AND OLIVIA SEARS, EDS.,
Best of Contemporary Mexican Fiction.
ELOY URROZ, *Friction.*
The Obstacles.
LUISA VALENZUELA, *He Who Searches.*
MARJA-LIISA VARTIO,
The Parson's Widow.
PAUL VERHAEGHEN, *Omega Minor.*
BORIS VIAN, *Heartsnatcher.*
LLORENÇ VILLALONGA, *The Dolls' Room.*
ORNELA VORPSI, *The Country Where No One Ever Dies.*
AUSTRYN WAINHOUSE, *Hedyphagetica.*
PAUL WEST,
Words for a Deaf Daughter & Gala.
CURTIS WHITE,
America's Magic Mountain.
The Idea of Home.
Memories of My Father Watching TV.
Monstrous Possibility: An Invitation to Literary Politics.
Requiem.
DIANE WILLIAMS, *Excitability:*
Selected Stories.
Romancer Erector.
DOUGLAS WOOLF, *Wall to Wall.*
Ya! & John-Juan.
JAY WRIGHT, *Polynomials and Pollen.*
The Presentable Art of Reading Absence.
PHILIP WYLIE, *Generation of Vipers.*
MARGUERITE YOUNG,
Angel in the Forest.
Miss MacIntosh, My Darling.
REYOUNG, *Unbabbling.*
VLADO ŽABOT, *The Succubus.*
ZORAN ŽIVKOVIĆ, *Hidden Camera.*
LOUIS ZUKOFSKY, *Collected Fiction.*
SCOTT ZWIREN, *God Head.*